Love Songs from the *Man'yōshū*

Personal Names Notice:
Japanese personal names are given surname first, the normal order
used in the Japanese language (e.g., Miyata Masayuki rather than
Masayuki Miyata). All other names appear in the Western order.

Originally published in 1989, in Japanese, under the title *Man'yō Koi-uta*
by Chūōkōronsha Ltd., Tokyo.

Book design by Point & Line

Distributed in the United States by Kodansha America, Inc., and in the United
Kingdom and continental Europe by Kodansha Europe Ltd.

Published by Kodansha International Ltd., 17-14, Otowa 1-chome, Bunkyo-ku,
Tokyo 112-8652, and Kodansha America, Inc.

First edition, 2000
10 09 08 07 06 05 04   10 9 8 7 6 5 4 3

www.thejapanpage.com

Love Songs
from the
Man'yōshū

SELECTIONS FROM A JAPANESE CLASSIC

宮田雅之 ［切り絵］
Illustrations by Miyata Masayuki

大岡　信 ［解説］
Commentary by Ōoka Makoto

リービ英雄 ［英訳］
Translation by Ian Hideo Levy

ドナルド・キーン ［エッセイ］
With an Essay by Donald Keene

KODANSHA INTERNATIONAL
Tokyo • New York • London

目次 ◆ CONTENTS

万葉恋歌
LOVE SONGS FROM THE MAN'YŌSHŪ

Preface for the English Reader

Ian Hideo Levy

The *Man'yōshū* is the first anthology of Japanese poetry. It is considered by many to be the greatest. The collection consists of over 4,500 poems, dating from the seventh and eight centuries A.D., the first golden age of Japanese culture. In its scale and breadth of expression, it ranks as one of the most important anthologies of lyric poetry in world literature.

As its title, "The Collection of Ten Thousand Leaves," suggests, this is the summation of literary expression in ancient Japan through the Nara period, what the Japanese court itself considered to be the cream of a century and more of poetry. It includes both works informed by a native Shintō sensibility and others which show a profound influence from the Asian Continent.

It is possible to roughly distinguish the poems of the *Man'yōshū* into "public" and "private" expressions. The "public" expressions largely deal with the imperial family, stately poems of praise for living emperors and elegies composed for imperial funerals. The "private" poems, by contrast, for the most part belong to the category known as "personal exchanges" (*sōmon*), most of them in the short *tanka* form of thirty-one syllables, which would later become the standard length of Japanese verse.

Here are to be found some of the most moving, passionate and witty poems ever exchanged between lovers in any language. The present book is a selection of some of the greatest poems from the "private" expressions, the eros and pathos of men and women who lived during the first flowering of a sophisticated culture in Japan.

One of the special characteristics of Japanese poetry, already apparent in the *Man'yōshū*, is its use of rich natural imagery to convey the delicate moods of the psyche as it interacts with the object of longing. Images both powerful and intricate are what give these verses their universal impact and are one factor which enables the translator to convey in contemporary English the emotions of Japanese lovers whose love thrived some twelve hundred years ago.

Along with the English translations here are dazzling visual "translations" by the late Miyata Masayuki, one of postwar Japan's most distinguished artists, and commentary by Ōoka Makoto, a leading poet who is also one of the foremost living interpreters of Japanese verse.

Here, then, is the erotic "core" of the Japanese sensibility as it found expression at the beginning of literary history—translated, interpreted and transformed into a contemporary visual art.

万葉集は新しい

リービ英雄

　日本語の作家になる前に、ぼくは長い間、日本語の読者であった。そしてときには日本語の文学作品を英語に翻訳することもあった。外から日本に越境して日本語で小説を書きはじめる前に、ぼくは日本語を外へ伝達する仕事にたずさわっていたのである。

　近代の小説や詩から始まって、それから日本では「古典文学」といわれている作品を読むようになった。段々さかのぼって、いつの間にか万葉集にたどりついた。そしてたどりついたとき、自分がもう一つの「現代文学」、あたかもきのう書かれたかのような新鮮なことばの世界に入りこんだ、という不思議な錯覚を経験した。1200年の時間がうそのように感じられて、まるで同時代の表現が目の前で展開されていると思わせるように、はじめて読んだ万葉集は、新しかった。

　1200年前に書かれた万葉集は、新しい。そして日本語がはじめて文学となった時代の感性は、おそらくは多くの近代日本人が考えてきた以上に、外国語に翻訳するとその本質的な何かが十分伝わるのだ。

　万葉集は、一つの大きな世界文学である。万葉集は、もしかすると、人類の古代から現代のぼくらに残されている最大の抒情詩集といえるかもしれない。シンプルのようで複合的な、島国文化で育った心情の「広」さ、そして大陸とは違ったことばの感触を、すべて集成した、4500首あまりの歌を収めた巨大な歌集を、読めば読むほど、この書物こそ現代の外国語に翻訳すべきものである、と考えるようになった。実際に万葉集を英訳してみて、そんな直感はけっしてまちがっていなかったことが分か

った。日本の「古典文学」の中で、これほど現代人の感性に直に響き合う作品はないし、日本語文学の長い伝統の中でもこれほど「外」の読者にも通じることばのタペストリーはない。

　自然現象の中から、読めば誰の心の目にも浮ぶはずの豊かなイメージをくみとり、それらのイメージを人間の根元的な心情を表すべく、何百何千もの清らかな歌のことばに結晶させる。何百何千もの視覚的な比喩を生み出す。一つ一つが実に鮮烈なイメージの表現なのである。そしてその力によって、7世紀と8世紀の日本語は、意外と21世紀の英語にも翻訳が可能となる。

　万葉集の中でも、恋の歌のように、日本文化の第一黄金時代を実際に生きたあの人たちの最もプライベートな心情をうったえた表現を日本語の外へ伝達しようとしたとき、翻訳には創作と同じぐらいのスリルと感動がある。

　本書はしかも、古代人のよろこびと悲しみに満ちたさまざまなプライベートな瞬間、エロスの微妙な動きを次々と輝けるヴィジュアル・アートに「翻訳」した宮田雅之氏の名作と、現代における詩歌解釈の第一人者である大岡信氏のコメントがあるので、英訳するという伝達のスリルは、多次元のそれとなった。

　1200年の歳月を越えて、現代人の心に響き合う、「世界文学」としての万葉集の新しさが、この本の中にある。

万葉逍遥

宮田雅之

「あしび」とはアセビのことである。漢字では馬酔木となるが、これはあしびが毒草で、馬が誤ってこの草を食べると、ふらふらと酒に酔ったような状態になることから来たものという。奈良の春日大社境内に樹齢数百年を経ると思われるあしびの密生した森があり、春ともなれば、ここはたわわに咲いた真白い花で覆われ、夢のような情緒に富む景観をなす。

奈良公園に放し飼いにされている神鹿は、あしびの毒を百も承知で、決して食べないと聞いた。口にすれば毒と知りつつ、その甘美な酔い心地に我を忘れて──咲き乱れた花の風情に何やら男女の官能の恋の宿命を思い起こし、1200年を遡る恋の美しさと哀しみに出合う私の万葉の旅は、このあしびの花から始まった。

恋。──それは人生において最も崇高で美しい体験──。男が女を、女が男を愛し、互いに求め合う恋の真理には、理屈や時代の差など問題にもならないであろう。それにしても何という大胆さ……。4500余首の万葉歌群の中から、さまざまな恋歌を撰び出していくと、古代東国人の素朴な東歌から、歴史に残る有名歌人の洗練された恋歌に至るまで、共通した眩いばかりの性の讃歌に出合う。戸惑うほど濃密で、大陸的な大らかさがあり、その享楽も官能も逞しく健康的で、自由奔放な開放感に満ち溢れている。その後の長い時代に我々が背負って来た性に対する屈折や翳りなど微塵もない。そこに生きている男女の心情や生活感覚は、どの時代よりも現代に近い。

Man'yō Promenade

Miyata Masayuki

The plant called *ashibi* in ancient Japanese is the modern *asebi*, the "Japanese andromeda." It is written with characters that mean "horse inebriation tree." The reason, it is said, is that the *ashibi* leaves are toxic, and when a horse mistakenly grazes on them it loses its footing and staggers as if drunk. In the precincts of the Grand Shrine of Kasuga, in Nara, is a forest with a rich growth of *ashibi*, believed to be hundreds of years old. When spring comes, the forest lies under a heavy covering of pure white blossoms which make for a scene of dreamlike, ethereal beauty.

I have heard that the sacred deer which roam freely in Nara Park are fully aware of the toxic nature of the *ashibi*, and won't touch it. To lose oneself in a sweet inebriation, knowing that one is taking in poison— from the raucous blossoming of those flowers—I imagined the fate of sensual love between man and woman. My personal *Man'yō* journey, an encounter with the beauty and pathos of a love which goes back 1,200 years, began with the *ashibi* blossom.

Love—the most sublime and beautiful experience in a person's life. The truth of longing—that a man loves a woman and a woman loves a man as they quest for each other, is not a matter of logic, is surely not limited to any particular period of history. And yet, what boldness we find here ... selecting various poems of love from among the more than 4,500 works in the *Man'yōshū*, we come across poems ranging from the simple and unadorned "Poems of the Eastland" to the sophisticated verses of poets whose names live on in history—all of them in praise of a dazzling sexuality. With a texture unnervingly dense, along with a "Continental" grandeur of emotion, its sensuality is stalwart and healthy, overflowing with an unrestrained freedom. There is not the slightest hint of shadow, not the slightest sign of that neurosis which would come to burden our consciousness of sex in the long

ある意味では現代よりもっと進歩的と言えるかもしれない。

　万葉人は男女が結婚しても、一緒に住むことをしない。その形態は「妻問い婚」で男が女のところに通って来る。結婚式や披露宴などの儀式的行事も一切やらないから、結婚と婚前との区別が今のようにはっきりしていない。結婚はお互いの意識の成就で決まり、行為が唯一の愛の証しとなる。一夫一婦制の咎（とが）めもないから、恋の対象が人妻であることも少なくない。「人妻に吾（あ）も交（まじ）はらむあが妻に人も言問（こと）へ」と余裕充分に人妻との恋の正当性を歌って、何ら悪びれるところがない。罪の意識どころかむしろ男は「──人妻故に我恋ひめやも」と、相手が人妻であるからこそ只管（ひたすら）その恋に執着し、女も「──この紐解（ひもと）けと言ふは誰（た）がこと」と豊満な色香を隠そうともせず、熟年の男女の恋の唱和は、高らかに繰り返されている。呆れるほど屈託のない正直な告白は、猥雑な感触など少しも感じさせない。むしろ微笑ましい思いで読み解くのである。

　過ぐる年「源氏物語」に取り組んだ時は、谷崎先生の現代語訳という力強い土台があった。画歴30周年記念の「おくのほそ道」では、自分で芭蕉の行程を歩いて確かめながら、事ある毎にドナルド・キーン先生の教えが助け船となった。今回の万葉集は私にとって手掛りを得るにも遠すぎる世界であったが、一昨年鑑真和上像を切り絵で再現する折、唐招提寺の森本長老に天平期の切り絵（紙に文様を切り抜いた素朴なものであったが）を見せていただいた時、黄ばんだ古紙の千切れた文様の一片が、不思議にも私の中で1200年という歴史的距離感を薄れさ

period of history to follow. The emotions and sense of life of these men and women are closer to our contemporary age than those of any other historical period. They may indeed be even more progressive than those of our age.

Men and women in the *Man'yōshū* period did not live together even after marriage. Their relationships took the form of "wife-visitation marriage," in which the man would commute to his wife's abode. Since there were no ceremonies at all, no weddings or banquets, the distinction between the pre- and post-nuptial state was not as clear as it is now. Marriage was a matter decided on the basis of the partners' consciousness; action was the sole proof of love. Lacking the censures of monogamy, love often found its objects in the wives of other men. "I shall keep company with the wife of another; let others make their proposals to my wife": thus was the propriety of extra-marital love generously sung, without the slightest hint of guilt. Far from being guilty, the man would become obsessed with a woman *because* "she was another man's wife," and the woman, wondering who it was who told her "to undo my waistcloth," made no attempt to conceal her own voluptuous emotions: thus were the recitations of love by mature men and women sonorously repeated. Their straightforward, astonishingly carefree confessions contain not the slightest suggestion of obscenity. If anything, we read them with an agreeable sense of bemusement.

Previously, when I was engaged on *The Tale of Genji*, I had the solid and powerful base of the great Tanizaki's modern translation to work from. And when I did *The Narrow Road to Oku*, commemorating my thirtieth anniversary as an artist, I was able to retrace Bashō's steps myself, and was helped by the teachings of Professor Donald Keene. When I first set out on the present project of the *Man'yōshū*, I found myself in a world so distant that I hardly had any clues to understanding it. Then the year before last, when I created an illustration of the Statue of Priest Ganjin, Elder Morimoto of the Tōshōdaiji Temple showed me some illustrations from the Tempyō period (simple works which consisted of designs cut

せた。すでにこの時代に切り絵らしきものがあったという事実が、新しい仕事にかかる時にありがちな過剰な身構えを取り去り、次第に万葉人を私に近づけてくれた。

　万葉歌は、万葉仮名と呼ぶさまざまな漢字をあてて書かれている。満天の星を数えるような恋歌の中で、「恋」を「孤悲」とあてた文字との出合いは、今回のすべての作品に通じる作画上の主題となった。万葉の抒情的唯美の頂点を象徴する二文字。目くるめく華麗な官能の恋歌に、この哀しいまでに美しい「孤悲」の文字が深みと彩りを添えておればこそ、万葉歌はひときわ瑞々しい光芒を放ち、1200年を経て今なお得難い美の典型を残したのであろう。

　三十一文字の中に恋する者の赤裸々な思いを結晶させ、詩魂のかぎりを尽して歌い残した万葉人の新鮮な恋愛美学の鮮度を、出来得るかぎりそのまま現代に伝えたいという主眼から、あえて色にも形にも抽象的な表現を避けた。

　　　若草の
　　　新手枕を
　　　まきそめて
　　　　夜をや隔てむ
　　　　憎くあらなくに

　新婚の妻に寄せる熱い想いを、惜し気もなく歌いあげた夫の歌である。この歌の意味する事実は現代にもある。しかし、この切実な思いを秘めた愛の絶唱は、今生まれ得ない。

out from paper). One of those crinkled and yellowed ancient slips of paper had the effect of reducing the distance, some 1,200 years, between me and that age. The fact that illustrations of this sort already existed in that period allowed me to relax my excessive guard as I set out on this new project, and gradually brought the people of the *Man'yō* age closer to me.

The *Man'yōshū* is written in a script of Chinese characters used various ways. The script is known as *Man'yōgana*. Among the poems on love, innumerable like the stars on a clear night, I encountered "love" written with characters which mean "solitary sadness," and from this encounter emerged a theme which is consistent throughout all the works in this book. The two characters symbolize the lyrical aesthetic of the *Man'yōshū* at its zenith. It is because this beautiful "solitary sadness" gives depth and color to the sensual expressions of love that such *Man'yō* poems emit a light of extraordinary freshness, and remain, after 1,200 years, as models of beauty yet unmatched. From a desire to transmit, to the greatest degree possible, the freshness and clarity of the aesthetic of love which the poets of the *Man'yō* age wrung from the spirit of poetry, crystallizing in thirty-one syllables the unreserved thoughts of those who love, I have deliberately avoided any abstract expressions of either color or form.

> Pillowed, for the first time,
> in the fresh new arms
> of a girl like the young grass:
> must there be intervals between such nights,
> though there be no disaffection?

The poem of a husband, in which he generously sings of his passion for his new wife. The *facts* which constitute the content of this poem exist in the present as well. But the cry of love in which these urgent feelings echo is one that cannot be born in our age.

宮田さんの切り絵

ドナルド・キーン

　宮田雅之さんの切り絵には美人画が多い。切り絵の曲線が、とくに美人の姿に向いているのかもしれないが、美人の顔や髪の毛や胸や腰や足が、宮田さんの刀によってみごとに描かれていて、忘れがたい色っぽさがある。もちろん、宮田さんの作品は美人画に限られてはいない。

　日本の風景、四季の花、近代小説の場面、宗教画（キリスト教）、わらべ歌、「おくのほそ道」の、それぞれの特徴を呼び起こさせる作品がある。

　今度の「万葉恋歌」の切り絵にも、美人が出ていない傑作がある。（中でも私は、久米朝臣広縄（ひろつな）の

　　　このしぐれ
　　　いたくな降りそ
　　　我妹子（わぎもこ）に
　　　　見せむがために
　　　　黄葉（もみち）取りてむ

をテーマにした切り絵がとくに好きである。）
　しかし、何と言っても宮田さんの美人画には特別の魅力がある。「おくのほそ道」の切り絵を作っておられた頃、芭蕉や曾良が美人と余りにも縁が少ないので、

　　　一つ家に
　　　遊女も寝たり
　　　萩と月

Miyata Masayuki's Paper Cut-Outs

Donald Keene

Many of Miyata Masayuki's paper cut-outs depict beautiful women. Perhaps this is because the curving lines of paper cut-outs are particularly suited to the natural curves of a beautiful woman. Be that as it may, the faces, hair, breasts, hips and legs of beautiful women, as so marvellously depicted by Mr. Miyata with his knife, leave an unforgettable impression of seductiveness.

Mr. Miyata's works include landscapes of Japan, flowers of the four seasons, scenes from modern novels, Christian religious themes, illustrations of children's songs and of Bashō's celebrated *The Narrow Road to Oku*, bringing out the special qualities of each.

There are also superb paper cut-outs in this collection of *Love Songs from the Man'yōshū* that do not depict beautiful women. (I am especially fond of the one that has for its theme the following poem by Kume Hirotsuna.)

> Autumn showers
> do not fall so hard,
> for I would pick the yellowing leaves
> and show them to my girl.

But it is hard to deny the special attraction of Mr. Miyata's portrayals of beautiful women. When he was making the cut-outs for *The Narrow Road to Oku*, there was so little connection between Bashō, his travelling companion Sora and beautiful women that he must have breathed a sigh of relief when he came to the haiku:

> Under the same roof
> prostitutes, too, were sleeping:
> clover and the moon.

という句の番となったとき、宮田さんはほっとしたことだろう。

　宮田さんの線のすばらしさには定評があるが、色彩の美もみごとなものである。黄葉の赤と黄と緑も、山桜花の薄いピンクや濃いピンクも美しいが、紺の空をバックにした真白な梅花も鮮やかである。また、高松塚の壁画を思わせる奈良朝の美人の服装は何とも言えない。どれを見ても綺麗であるが、

　　　　振分の
　　　　　髪を短み
　　　　青草を
　　　　　　髪にたくらむ
　　　　　妹をしそ思ふ

に基づいた切り絵の若妻は髪ばかりでなく、美しい衣装で男の視線を引く。家持の

　　　　春の苑
　　　　　くれなゐにほふ
　　　　桃の花
　　　　　した照る道に
　　　　　出で立つをとめ

の切り絵の女性の身体も、長いスカートも、桃の木に融け込むようになっており、桃の花の色と美人の衣装がみごとに調和している。この女性はギリシア神話に出るドリュアスという木に住む木の精であろう。宮田さんは線と色彩の美によって神話の世界を描き出した。

　源氏絵にしても、わらべ歌を体現した作品にしても、万葉の時代を伝える切り絵にしても、美人が着る服装がそれぞれ違う。「万葉恋歌」の女性美の最も顕著なところは髪の毛と衣服であろう。キモノと相当違う、仙女が

The remarkable beauty of Mr. Miyata's lines has long since been acknowledged, but his use of color is also extraordinary. The red, yellow and green of maple leaves and the pale or dark pink of mountain cherry blossoms are beautiful, but pure white plum blossoms against a deep blue sky also form a brilliant contrast. Again, words cannot describe the costumes of the beautiful women of the Nara Period, recalling the frescoes in the Takamatsuzuka tombs. All of them are lovely, but the young woman in the paper cut-out based on the following poem attracts a man's gaze not only by her hair but by her beautiful costume:

> My thoughts are of my girl:
> her hair, parted in the middle,
> is too short to be raised and tied
>> like a woman's,
> and so in it she bundles green leaves.

The body of the woman in the paper cut-out illustrating the poem by Ōtomo no Yakamochi

> In the spring garden
> the crimson is lustrous;
> girl who appears
> standing on the path
> beneath the gleam of peach blossoms.

and the long skirt she wears both seem to melt into the peach tree, and the color of the peach blossoms wonderfully harmonizes with the costume of the beautiful woman. Perhaps she is a spirit who lives in the tree, like the dryads who appear in Greek myths. Mr. Miyata has with his lines and colors evoked the world of myths.

The costumes worn by the beautiful women who appear in Mr. Miyata's representations of *The Tale of Genji* or in the works inspired by children's songs, as well as in the paper cut-outs of the age of the *Man'yōshū,* all wear different costumes, depending on the period. The

着るような服装は異国的に見え、奈良朝という中国崇拝の時代を伝える。

　宮田さんは絵の人物の衣装の色や柄を定める前に、きっと古い文献や絵を丹念に調べたと思う。山上憶良の

　　　彦星し
　　　　妻迎へ舟
　　　漕ぎ出らし
　　　　天の川原に
　　　　霧の立てるは

という歌にインスピレーションを受けた切り絵に現れる美人の髪の毛や服装ばかりでなく、扇の模様まで中国的であり、彼女が坐っている雲も、いかにも中国的な雲である。また、彦星の船も遣唐使が乗ったような船である。天の川を渡るために出来た船にふさわしく、いかにも軽々と夜の空を横切っている。

「万葉恋歌」の宮田さんの切り絵を鑑賞するには、特別な知識等はまったく不要である。誰でもこれらの美しい絵に魅惑されてしまう。が、万葉時代の歌人たちが描こうとした世界の本質をとらえることは芸術家のしわざであり、宮田雅之さんはそういう芸術家である。

most striking feature of the beautiful women of *Love Songs from the Man'yōshū* is their hair and their robes. The clothes, quite unlike modern kimonos, are more suited to fairies than to mortal women, and suggested the worship of Chinese civilization that was a feature of the Nara period.

No doubt Mr. Miyata, before deciding on the colors and patterns of the costumes worn by the figures in his works, carefully studied old documents and paintings of the period. In the case of the beautiful woman who appears in the paper cut-out inspired by the poem of Yamanoue Okura

> It seems that the herd boy
> has begun rowing his boat
> across the sky to meet his wife:
> the mist is rising
> on the riverbank of heaven.

not only are her hair and her costume Chinese, but so too is the design on the fan she carries. The cloud on which she sits is also a very Chinese-looking cloud. The herd boy's boat recalls the ships aboard which Japanese travelled to China. Appropriately for a boat which was made to cross the Milky Way, this boat crosses the night sky ever so lightly.

No special knowledge of the background is required to appreciate Mr. Miyata's paper cut-outs for *Love Songs from the Man'yōshū*. Anyone who looks at them is sure to be captivated by their beauty. But capturing the essence of the world which the poets of the age of the *Man'yōshū* were attempting to portray is the task of an artist. Mr. Miyata is that kind of artist.

解説序文

大岡　信

　　私たちは生涯のある量の時間を、どういうわけでか本
を読むことに費やす。その中には生活必需品と同じ意味
で読まねばならない本も多少は含まれるが、本を読む醍
醐味はむしろ、読まなくてもいい本を発見して、あたか
も解き放たれた夢の中のような気分で読む所にある。
『万葉集』という日本古代 7 世紀前半から約130年間の
歌を集めた本は、そういう意味ではなかなか面白い夢を
見させてくれる集である。これを単に大昔の本とだけ思
ったらまちがいだろう。ここには、恋愛の歌だけとって
見ても、乙女のういういしい素朴な愛から、成熟した女
の遊戯的な、あるいは醒めて達観した愛にいたるまで、
思いがけないほどの広がりを見せる、退屈ならざる世界
がある。
　　実際、現代人が読んでも十分自らの中に手応えを感じ
うるのが万葉の世界である。宮田雅之氏はそのような現
代的な立場に立って自由に想像力をはばたかせ、いわば
宮田版万葉びとの世界を切り絵によって描きだそうとす
る。鋭利で精緻な刀さばきのもと、宮田スタイルの女た
ちのほっそりした胴、切れ長のまなざしに、独特のエロ
ティシズムの黙劇を演じさせようとしているのである。

A Word about the Commentary

Ōoka Makoto

For some reason we expend a portion of the time allotted us in life in the reading of books. These include a certain number of books that we read as a kind of practical necessity. But the truly great reading experiences come from our discovery of books that we indeed *don't* have to read, books that liberate us, release us into a state like a free-floating dream.

In that sense the *Man'yōshū*, a compilation of poetry from a 130-year period stretching from the beginning of the seventh century A.D., is a book which reveals to us very interesting dreams. It would be a mistake to see this as merely a book of great antiquity. Taking just the love poems from the anthology, one finds an endlessly stimulating world, a realm of astonishing breadth, ranging from the fresh and unaffected love of young maidens to the gamelike, or the ironic and knowing love of mature women.

In fact, the world of the *Man'yōshū* is one with a full and personal resonance for the modern reader as well. The artist Miyata Masayuki, taking such a contemporary perspective—his imagination free and soaring— has here expressed through his paper cut-out illustrations the inhabitants of a world which constitutes the "Miyata *Man'yōshū*." In the slender torsos and the glances of the long-slitted eyes of these Miyata-style women, he has produced a silent drama of unique eroticism.

Love Songs from the *Man'yōshū*

あかねさす紫野行き標野行き野守は見ずや君が袖振る

額田王

Akane sasu
murasaki-no yuki
shime-no yuki
nomori wa mizu ya
kimi ga sode furu

Going over the fields of murasaki grass
that shimmer crimson,
going over the fields marked as imperial domain,
will the guardian of the fields not see you
as you wave your sleeves at me?

Princess Nukata

あかねさす
紫野行き
標野(しめの)行き
　野守(もり)は見ずや
　君が袖(そで)振る

額田 王(ぬかたの おおきみ)
［巻1・20］

1　「紫草の群生する野を行き、御料地（標野）を行き、なんと大胆なお方、野の番人は見とがめないでしょうか、私に袖を振って合図していらっしゃるあなたを」

　万葉の恋歌といえばまずこの歌、と決めている人も多いだろう。開巻まもなく出てくるので一層印象が強い。この歌に対して、手を振った当の人である大海人皇子(おおあまのみこ)の歌が次に出ている。

紫草(むらさき)の
にほへる妹(いも)を
憎くあらば
　人妻ゆゑに
　我恋ひめやも

　今は人妻になっているかつてのわが妻に贈った恋歌である。近代以後なら当然そこに三角関係を想像することであろう。前夫の大海人皇子と、現在の夫たる天智天皇の二人の間で揺れ動く女ごころ、それが大海人に向けたこの歌の中にある——そう読んで胸ときめかした人々も多い。

　しかしそういう三角関係的な秘話は残念ながら古代のこの男女の関係には当てはまらない。でも、それはそれでいいではないか。この歌、音調はいいし内容は心そそるし、それに大海人の彼女を讃える返歌も打てば響くようについていて、2首相まってめでたい恋歌なのだ。

Going over the fields of murasaki grass

that shimmer crimson,

going over the fields marked as imperial domain,

will the guardian of the fields not see you

as you wave your sleeves at me?

Princess Nukata
[Volume 1, 20]

Many people consider this the greatest love poem in the *Man'yōshū*. The impression it gives is all the more powerful as it appears near the beginning of the anthology. Following this poem is one by Prince Ōama, the man who waved his sleeves at Princess Nukata.

If I despised you, who are as beautiful

as the murasaki grass,

would I be longing for you like this,

though you are another man's wife?

This is a love poem sent to a former wife who is now someone else's wife. The modern reader of course imagines a triangular relationship. The heart of a woman is torn between her former husband, Prince Ōama, and her present husband, Emperor Tenchi, and her ambivalence is expressed in the poem to Ōama. Many contemporary readers are excited by such a reading.

Unfortunately, such concepts of a love triangle do not fit with the actual relationships between men and women in the ancient age. But that, too, does not matter. This poem has a graceful melody and a content that stirs the emotions, and the poem which follows it echoes back with Ōama's praise of the princess. The two poems, coupled, create a most auspicious expression of love.

春の苑くれなゐにほふ桃の花した照る道に出で立つをとめ　大伴家持

Haru no sono
kurenai niou
momo no hana
shitateru michi ni
idetatsu otome

In the spring garden

the crimson is lustrous;

girl who appears

standing on the path

beneath the gleam of peach blossoms.

Ōtomo Yakamochi

春の苑(その)

くれなゐにほふ

桃の花

　した照る道に

　出で立つをとめ

大伴家持(おおとものやかもち)
［巻19・4139］

2　正倉院の「鳥毛立女図屏風」その他、「樹下美人」を描いた古代の絵が日本にも現存する。インドにも中国にもきわめて古くからある図柄で、日本のは唐風の女性風俗をした天平美人だ。樹下の霊的な生命力はとりわけ女性に似つかわしく感じられたのかもしれない。

　家持34歳当時、国守として赴任していた越中で、自邸の庭の桃と李の花、つまり紅白2種の花をながめて作った2首のうち、これは桃の歌。「にほふ」は紅に照り輝く。天平勝宝2年3月1日（今の4月10日すぎ）、桃の花は満開で、木陰までも照り映えている。ふとそこに立つ乙女。現実の女か、桃の精か。空想かと思わせるほどに、万葉でも異色の華やかな花と女の図。

In the spring garden
the crimson is lustrous;
girl who appears
standing on the path
beneath the gleam of peach blossoms.

Ōtomo Yakamochi
[Volume 19, 4139]

In Japan, as in other Asian countries, there are paintings from the ancient period depicting a "beautiful woman beneath a tree." One example is the feather-decorated "Screen Panels with Women under a Tree" in the Shōsō-in repository in Nara. Such themes were present in the visual arts in China and India since ancient times; the works extant in Japan depict "Tempyō beauties," women attired in the styles of Tang Dynasty China. Perhaps a spiritual vitality in the shade of the trees was perceived as an especially appropriate way of portraying women.

Yakamochi was thirty-four years old at the time. Residing in the province of Etchu, where he had been posted as governor, he composed a pair of poems upon viewing the peach and damson blossoms (flowers that bloomed in red and white respectively) in his garden. This is the poem on the peach blossoms. The word *niou* in the original refers to a crimson-colored gleam. On the first day of the third lunar month (corresponding to sometime after the tenth of April) in 750 A.D., the peach flowers were in full blossom, their gleam reaching even the shade of the trees. Suddenly there is a girl standing there. A real girl or a peach nymph? Even among the works of the *Man'yōshū* this gorgeous portrayal of blossom and woman is so extraordinary as to make us wonder whether the entire scene wasn't the poet's fantasy.

この花の一（ひと）よの内（うち）に百種（ももくさ）の言（こと）そ隠（こも）れるおほろかにすな

藤原朝臣広嗣（ふじわらのあそんひろつぐ）

Kono hana no
hitoyo no uchi ni
momo-kusa no
koto so komoreru
ooroka ni suna

In a single sprig

of these blossoms

are concealed a hundred words;

do not treat me lightly.

Fujiwara Hirotsugu

この花の
一よの内に
百種の
　言そ隠れる
　おほろかにすな

藤原朝臣広嗣
[巻8・1456]

3　「一よ」（原文・一与）は他に用例がない語で、花びらの
一弁の意かとも一枝の意かともいう。いずれにせよ、桜
の花の枝を折り、この歌をその枝に結いつけて、さる乙
女に贈ったのである。

「この花のひとひらのうちに、さまざまのことばが隠っ
ているのだ。あだおろそかに思ってくれるな」。もちろ
ん求愛の歌。

　季節季節に咲く美しい花に恋歌を結びつけて贈る床し
い風習は、すでに奈良時代からあったことがわかる。こ
の歌の相手の乙女が返した歌も可憐。こういうのだ。
「枝が折られたのは、きっと一ひらの中にそんなに多く
の言葉をかかえきれなかったからかしら」

　心はイエスと言おうとしている。しかし言葉はまだた
めらっているのである。

In a single sprig
of these blossoms
are concealed a hundred words;
do not treat me lightly.

Fujiwara Hirotsugu
[Volume 8, 1456]

This is the sole extant example of the word *hitoyo*, translated here as "a single sprig." It apparently refers to either a single petal or a single sprig of blossoms. In either case, the poet plucked off a branch of cherry blossoms, tied his poem to it, and sent it to a young girl. Of course it is a courting poem.

Here we see that the admirable custom of attaching love poems to the flowers which blossom in each season was already established in the Nara period. The poem that the girl addressed here sent in response is touching too. It says that the reason the sprig is bent is that it couldn't support all the words it contains.

The heart longs to say yes. But language still hesitates.

春さればしだり柳のとををにも妹は心に乗りにけるかも

柿本朝臣人麻呂歌集

Haru sareba
shidari-yanagi no
tooo nimo
imo wa kokoro ni
norinikeru kamo

Like the lithe bending

of the weeping willows

when spring arrives,

so my woman has set herself upon my soul,

bending it, pliantly.

From the Kakinomoto Hitomaro Collection

春されば
しだり柳の
とををにも
　妹は心に
　乗りにけるかも

柿本朝臣人麻呂歌集
　　　　　　　　　　［巻10・1896］

4　　いとしいと思う女が自分の心を占めてしまってどうに
もならないほどだ、ということを言うのに、「妹は心に
乗りにけるかも」とは何とも心にくい表現である。

　心なんてものは目に見えず、またその動きだってほん
とは逐一追跡することさえできない。けれど、一人のし
なやかな軀幹の女が心の上に乗ってしまった、と言われ
れば、その心はにわかに目にも見え、手にも触れうるも
のになる。詩の言葉の恐ろしさがそこにある。

　「春されば」は春ともなると。サルは移る意だが、行く
のにも来るのにも言った。「とをを」は撓むさまで、タ
ワワの母音が変化した形。春のしだれ柳がしなうよう
に、私の心もしなうほど、しなやかなお前が……

Like the lithe bending
of the weeping willows
when spring arrives,
so my woman has set herself upon my soul,
bending it, pliantly.

From the Kakinomoto Hitomaro Collection
[Volume 10, 1896]

In order to convey that situation in which a beloved woman has captured his heart and rendered him helpless, the poet uses words which literally mean "she has mounted my soul." What a unique expression this is!

The soul is a thing invisible to the eye, and its workings cannot be traced through any physical expression. But when we are told that a lithe-bodied woman has mounted or set herself upon the soul, we perceive a glimmer of that soul, and sense it in a tangible way. This is the awesome and frightful power of poetry.

The words *haru sareba* in the original refer to the coming of spring. The verb *saru* refers to a shift; it can mean either "to come" or "to go." *Tooo* in the original refers to a state of litheness or pliancy. Like the lithe bending of the weeping willows, so my heart bends pliantly, as you with your lithe body . . .

妹に似る草と見しより我が標めし野辺の山吹誰か手折りし

大伴家持

Imo ni niru
kusa to mishiyori
wa ga shimeshi
nohe no yamabuki
tare ka taorishi

Ever since I saw in it

a resemblance to you, my woman,

I marked off the kerria grass on the field—

now someone has plucked it.

Ōtomo Yakamochi

妹に似る

草と見しより

我が標めし

　野辺の山吹

　誰か手折りし

大伴家持
［巻19・4197］

5　代作という行為は、現代の感覚だと多少うさん臭く思われる。人の書くものはその人以外の誰のものでもない唯一絶対のものだ、という窮屈な自我中心の思想が近代思想を覆ったからだった。しかし古代人はそんな気兼ねなしに代作をしたし、また依頼もした。別人に成り代って歌を作り文を綴ることは、その心得のある人間にとってはむしろ喜ばしい腕の見せ所でもあった。

　この歌も実は代作。越中守として越中の国庁にあった家持が、妻に代って、故郷の奈良にいる女性（家持の妹）にあててこの歌をつくって贈ったのである。元来は家持の妻あてに妹から来た手紙があり、この歌はそれにこたえて送ったもの。山吹が出てくるのは、相手から先にきた歌に山吹の花が詠まれていたためである。しかしそんな事情を抜きにして読めば、これもまた万葉の恋歌と読めるし、いっそその方がすっきり読めさえする。「標めし」は自分の所有であると目印をしておくことなのだから。

Ever since I saw in it
a resemblance to you, my woman,
I marked off the kerria grass on the field—
now someone has plucked it.

Ōtomo Yakamochi
[Volume 19, 4197]

The act of surrogate composition, writing in place of someone else, somehow seems false to contemporary sensibilities. This is because modern thought is permeated with a sense of the self as absolute: what a person writes is his and his alone. How tiresomely self-centered such modern thought is. In contrast, the ancients composed in place of others without a second thought, and with the same freedom they requested others to compose for them. To become the other and create poetry or write prose for him was, for a creator with understanding, an act to take delight in, a display of one's true skill.

The above poem is such a surrogate composition. Yakamochi, who had been posted to the province of Etchū as governor, wrote it in place of his wife and sent it to a woman (Yakamochi's sister) in the capital at Nara. The poem is a response to a letter sent from the sister to Yakamochi's wife. It refers to the kerria grass because the flowers of the kerria were mentioned in the poem which came with the letter. But if we consider the poem apart from that fact, it reads very much like a *Man'yō* love poem, and in fact makes even better sense when read that way. For "to mark" is here to establish as one's possession.

松浦川川の瀬速み紅の裳の裾濡れて鮎か釣るらむ　大伴旅人

Matsuragawa
kawa-no-se hayami
kurenai no
mo no suso nurete
ayu ka tsururan

Quick are the rapids

in the Matsura River;

do the maidens wet the hems

of their crimson robes

as they catch the sweetfish there?

Ōtomo Tabito

松浦川
まつらがは

川の瀬速み

紅の
くれなゐ

　裳の裾濡れて
　も　　すそぬ

　鮎か釣るらむ
　あゆ

大伴旅人
おほとものたびと
［巻5・861］

6

　松浦川というのは北九州玄界灘に臨む景勝の地唐津湾に流れこんでいる川である。県でいえば佐賀県東松浦郡。大伴旅人は晩年の一時期、大宰府長官として今の福岡県太宰府に起居した。下僚には山上憶良をはじめ天平時代の代表的な知識人の一群がいて、ときに詩歌を作り合ったりする文芸サロンも旅人のもとで開催された。

　そういう雰囲気のなかでいちばん人気があったのは、海のかなたの大国唐の詩や小説。『遊仙窟』のような仙境の物語は、現実離れした空想世界の魅力、そこに現れるえもいわれぬ美女のあやかしのおかげで、後進国たるヤマトのインテリさんたちの胸を焦がした。

　この歌は、松浦川に遊んでそんな女たちに出会ったという想定のもとに作られた歌物語の1首。叙景と叙情がうまく嚙み合って、「紅の裳の裾」を濡らして鮎を釣っているらしい乙女の姿が鮮やかである。空想の歌だったから、作者も一層生き生きとその世界にとびこんでいる。

Quick are the rapids
in the Matsura River;
do the maidens wet the hems
of their crimson robes
as they catch the sweetfish there?

Ōtomo Tabito
[Volume 5, 861]

The Matsura River flows into the scenic Karatsu Bay in northern Kyūshū. In contemporary Japan, this is Matsura County, Saga Prefecture. In his later years, Ōtomo Tabito served as Commander of the Dazaifu, located in the present Fukuoka Prefecture, also in northern Kyūshū. Serving under him was a group of some of the most prominent intellectuals of the Tempyō period, including the great Yamanoue Okura. It was Tabito who organized the literary salon there, in which exchanges were made of Chinese and Japanese poetry.

In this milieu, the most popular literary works were the poems and romances of Tang China, the great country that lay across the sea. Stories of magical lands, such as *The Dwelling of Playful Goddesses*, fired the imagination of the intellectuals of the backward country Yamato with their depictions of imaginary worlds far from reality, worlds in which enchantingly beautiful women appeared.

The above poem comes from a narrative series of poetry describing an imaginary encounter with such fantasy women during a sojourn to the Matsura River. The description and the lyrical emotion play well together, and the figures the maidens make as they catch the sweetfish, drenching "the hems of their crimson robes," are dazzling. Because it was an imagined situation, the poet fashioned his world with all the more vividness.

青山を横ぎる雲のいちしろく我と笑まして人に知らゆな

大伴坂上郎女

Aoyama o
yokogiru kumo no
ichishiroku
ware to emashite
hito ni shirayuna

Do not let men find out

by smiling at me so apparently,

like the clouds that clearly cross

over the verdant mountains.

Lady Ōtomo Sakanoue

青山を

横ぎる雲の

いちしろく

我と笑まして

人に知らゆな

大伴坂上郎女
［巻4・688］

7 「いちしろく」という語は耳慣れないが、イチジルシク
というのなら誰でも知っている。前者が元の形である。
きわだって、顕著にという意味。

　つまりこの歌の上句は、青々と草木の茂る山を横ぎっ
て通る雲がきわだって鮮明なように、と形容する序詞と
して用いられている句で、何にかかるかといえば下句の
「笑む」動作にかかる。女が恋人に言っているのである、
「私にむかって目立つように頬笑みかけたりして、人に
知られるようなこと、しないで下さいね」と。

　「我と」は原文「吾共」で、私に向かってという意味。
この作者は万葉女性歌人中最も多くの歌が集にのってい
る魅力ある才女だったが、女ごころの多彩な表現でもイ
チシロキ女性だった。

Do not let men find out
by smiling at me so apparently,
like the clouds that clearly cross
over the verdant mountains.

Lady Ōtomo Sakanoue
[Volume 4, 688]

The ancient word *ichishiroku*, "clearly" or "apparently," may be unfamiliar to the contemporary Japanese reader. But it is the original form of the modern word *ichijirushiku*, "remarkably."

The first three lines of the original, "so apparently, like the clouds that clearly cross over the verdant mountains," are employed as a prelude to introduce the gesture "by smiling" in the fourth line (the order is reversed in the English translation). A woman is telling her lover, Don't smile at me in a way that will be apparent to other people.

The author was a woman of immense talent and charm, whose works are more numerous than any other woman poet of the *Man'yōshū*. In her multivaried expressions of female emotions, she was also a "remarkable" woman.

人妻に言ふは誰がことさ衣のこの紐解けと言ふは誰がこと

読人不詳

Hitozuma ni
iu wa tagakoto
sa-goromo no
kono himo toke to
iu wa tagakoto

Whose words are these,

spoken to the wife of another?

Whose words are these,

that bade me untie

the sash of my robe?

Anonymous

人妻に
言ふは誰がこと
さ衣の
　この紐解けと
言ふは誰がこと

読人不詳
［巻12・2866］

8　「こと」は「言」で、言葉の意。これは人妻の立場に立
って、言い寄る男に向かって言っているのである。
　「わたしは人妻よ。そのわたしに向かって、着物の下紐
を解けと言うのはどなたのおことば？」という意味だが、
「誰がこと」を2回繰返しているところに、民謡的な軽
やかさと明かるさがある。作者不詳の歌は万葉集のきわ
めて重要な部分をなしているが、その中には民謡として
愛誦されたにちがいない歌がたくさんある。
　さてこの歌は女性の作った歌だろうか。私にはとても
そうは思われない。男が作って男どもが愛誦した歌にち
がいない。「人妻」は性の願望の対象としての人妻で、
万葉のうたびとたちは人妻との秘密の恋のテーマに特別
の愛着を示した。

Whose words are these,

   spoken to the wife of another?

Whose words are these,

     that bade me untie

      the sash of my robe?

Anonymous
[Volume 12, 2866]

The poem is written from the perspective of "the wife of another," responding to the words of a man who has approached her.

In the repetition of the phrase *tagakoto,* "whose words are these?" one senses the brightness and buoyancy of a folk song. Anonymous poems constitute an important part of the *Man'yōshū*; many of them were folk songs which had been lovingly recited.

Was this poem written by a woman? I strongly doubt it. Surely a man composed it, and it was popularly recited by men. "The wife of another" was an object of male sexual desire; the poets of the *Man'yōshū* showed a special attachment to the theme of secret love with the wives of other men.

見渡せば明石（あかし）の浦に燭（とも）す火のほにそ出（い）でぬる妹（いも）に恋ふらく

門部王（かどべのおおきみ）

Miwataseba
Akashi no ura ni
tomosu hi no
ho niso idenuru
imo ni kouraku

Gazing out,

I see the fires that fishermen have lit

in Akashi Cove,

like the longing for my woman

that has flared from me.

Prince Kadobe

見渡せば
明石の浦に
燭す火の
　ほにそ出でぬる
　妹に恋ふらく

門部王
［巻3・326］

9　門部王が難波の海辺で漁師のいさり火を見て作った歌、と詞書にはあるが、歌の真意は船のともし火の景色などにはなく、女性への恋の告白にある。

「見渡せば明石の浦に燭す火の」までは、次の「ほに出づ」（表面にあらわれる、目につくようになる）を引き出すための序なのである。つまりこれは、今まで隠していた恋ごころが、ついに人目にまでつくようになってしまった、ということで、おそらく女にあてての求愛の手紙そのものだったのではないか。

上句の美しい叙景が、それゆえ一層よき伴奏の効果を発揮するわけだ。作者は貴族仲間でも風流人として名高かったという。なお「ほ」は稲の穂、波の秀など、突き出ていて人目に立つものをいう。

Gazing out,

I see the fires that fishermen have lit

    in Akashi Cove,

like the longing for my woman

that has flared from me.

Prince Kadobe
[Volume 3, 326]

The headnote to this poem tells us it was written by Prince Kadobe as he stood on the Naniwa seashore and saw the lights of fishermen. However, the true meaning of the poem lies not in its description of the lights but in its confession of love to a woman.

The phrase "Gazing out, I see the fires that fishermen have lit in Akashi Cove," is a prelude which introduces the words *ho ni izu*, "to appear prominently," here translated as "to flare." In other words, a yearning that has remained hidden has here suddenly become visible and apparent. It is possible that this poem itself constituted the Prince's missive declaring his love, and for this reason, the beautiful description perfectly echoes the content of the poem. It is said that the poet was famous as a man of great elegance in his aristocratic circle. The word *ho* refers to things that are prominent and apparent to the eye: the ears of rice plants, the crests of waves.

昼は咲き夜は恋ひ寝る合歓木の花君のみ見めや戯奴さへに見よ　紀女郎

Hiru wa saki
yoru wa koinuru
nebu no hana
kimi nomi mimeya
wake saeni miyo

The silk-tree flower that blooms in the day

closes as it sleeps,

yearning through the night.

Should only its lord look upon it?

You too, my vassal, enjoy the sight.

Lady Ki

昼は咲き
夜（よる）は恋ひ寝（ね）る
合歓木（ねぶ）の花
君のみ見めや
戯奴（わけ）さへに見よ

紀女郎（きのいらつめ）
［巻8・1461］

10　古代の男女関係には、なかなか味（あじ）なことをやってると思わせられるものがある。天平の盛時ともなれば、少なくとも上流階級の男女間の消息のかわしかたには、現代人顔負けのウィットに富んだ恋歌の交換があった。

紀女郎は安貴王（あきのおおきみ）の妻だったが、王が不敬罪によって失脚したのち、万葉末期の大歌人大伴家持と親しくなったらしい。この歌は彼女が家持に、花と一緒に贈った歌の1首。

「これは昼間は咲き、夜になると恋をしながら寝るという合歓木（ねぶ）の花ですよ。ご主人様だけで見て楽しむのはもったいない。これ、そちも見て楽しみなさい」

「ご主人様」とはすなわち紀女郎自身。「そち」とは相手の家持。現実の地位からすれば、もちろん大伴家の主人家持の方が上。男と女の世界では、身分上の上下関係は簡単に乗り越えられる。

The silk-tree flower that blooms in the day
closes as it sleeps,
yearning through the night.
Should only its lord look upon it?
You too, my vassal, enjoy the sight.

Lady Ki
[Volume 8, 1461]

There is often something quite piquant about relations between men and women in the ancient period. When the sophisticated Tempyō culture was at its peak, one saw a degree of wit in the exchange of love poems which puts us moderns to shame.

Lady Ki was the wife of Prince Aki, but after the prince lost his position through an act of *lèse-majesté*, she became familiar with the great late-*Man'yō* poet Ōtomo Yakamochi. This is a poem which she sent to Yakamochi along with a present of blossoms.

The "lord" here refers to Lady Ki herself. The "you" addressed here is Yakamochi. Of course, in actual rank, Yakamochi, the scion of the great Ōtomo house, was above her. In the world of men and women, hierarchies were transcended with ease.

夏の野の繁（しげ）みに咲ける姫（ひめ）百（ゆり）合（り）の知らえぬ恋は苦しきものそ　大伴坂上郎女（おおとものさかのうえのいらつめ）

Natsu no no no
shigemi ni sakeru
hime-yuri no
shiraenu koi wa
kurushiki mono so

Painful is the love

that remains unknown to the beloved,

like the star lily that has bloomed

in the thick foliage

of the summer field.

Lady Ōtomo Sakanoue

夏の野の
繁みに咲ける
姫百合の
　知らえぬ恋は
　苦しきものそ

　　　　　　　大 伴 坂 上 郎 女
　　　　　　　　　　　［巻8・1500］

11　　国語辞典で「姫百合」を引けばまず必ずといっていい
ほどこの歌が文例として引用されている。歌も可憐だ
が、古代の文献に見える姫百合としてはこれがたぶん最
も古いと認められているからだろう。

　けれどこの歌の中では、姫百合は相手に知られぬ片思
いをしている乙女の、その苦しい恋の比喩として使われ
ているので、姫百合そのものを対象にした歌ではない。
こういうレトリックは古代日本の和歌ではそれなりに大
いに発達していた。この歌の場合上三句が「知らえぬ」
にかかる比喩で、これを序詞という。

　この歌、万葉女流中の大立物の作だが、余裕ある作風
からみると、うぶな乙女のための代作のような気もする。
郎女はそんな作でも上手な人だった。「夏の野の草花の
繁みにつつましく咲いている姫百合、その花同様人知れ
ぬひそかな恋は、ほんとうに苦しいものなのですよ」

Painful is the love
that remains unknown to the beloved,
like the star lily that has bloomed
in the thick foliage
of the summer field.

Lady Ōtomo Sakanoue
[Volume 8, 1500]

The entry for "*hime-yuri*" (star lily, literally "maiden lily") in any Japanese dictionary includes, almost without exception, this poem as a usage example. The poem itself is a touching one, but more than that, it is generally recognized by scholars as containing the earliest appearance of the word "*hime-yuri*" in an ancient text.

In this poem, however, the star lily itself is not described; rather, it is employed as a metaphor for the pain experienced by a young girl whose unrequited longing remains unknown to its object. This sort of rhetoric is highly developed in ancient Japanese *waka* poetry. In this particular poem, the first three lines constitute a metaphor of "unknownness." This device is called a *joshi* or "prelude."

Although by one of the greatest women poets of the *Man'yōshū*, this work shows a stylistic composure which suggests it was written as a surrogate expression for an inexperienced young girl. The Lady was skilled at such compositions.

高麗錦紐の片方ぞ床に落ちにける明日の夜し来なむと言はば取り置きて待たむ

柿本朝臣人麻呂歌集

Koma-nishiki
himo no katae zo
toko ni ochinikeru
asu no yoshi
kinan to iwaba
toriokite matan

One of the sashes of Korean brocade

that, in our vow, we tied together

has come undone and fallen to the floor.

If you promise to visit me when night returns

I shall keep it, awaiting you.

From the Kakinomoto Hitomaro Collection

高麗錦（こまにしき）
紐の片方ぞ（ひも かた へ）
床に落ちにける（とこ）
　明日の夜し（あ す よ）
　来なむと言はば（き）
　取り置きて待たむ

柿本朝臣人麻呂歌集（かきのもとのあ そん ひと ま ろ）
［巻11・2356］

12

　五七七を二度くりかえす詩形で、旋頭歌（せどうか）という。女が一夜を共寝した相手の男にむかって、暁方、彼が立ち去る寸前に言うのである。

　「下着の高麗錦の紐の片方が床に落ちていたわ。でも今はあなたにあげない。今夜またやってくるとおっしゃるなら、私の所に取っておいてあなたを待つわ」

　日が落ちてから男が女を訪れ、夜明けとともに立ち去る妻問い婚の場合、こういう歌に見られる女ごころは、たぶんごく一般的だっただろう。それを嬉しがる男もいたろうが、紐を質にとられてしまったと嘆く浮気男もまたいたろう。

　高麗錦は高麗舶来の錦。してみればこの男、裕福な上流階級の人物像。歌は人麻呂歌集に採録された当時の流行歌のたぐいか。

One of the sashes of Korean brocade
that, in our vow, we tied together
has come undone and fallen to the floor.
If you promise to visit me when night returns
I shall keep it, awaiting you.

From the Kakinomoto Hitomaro Collection
[Volume 11, 2356]

This is a poetic form called the *sedōka*, which consists of two triplets in 5-7-7 syllabic rhythm. Here a woman who has spent the night with a man addresses him as he is about to leave the next morning at dawn. She tells him that she will not return his brocade sash now, but will keep it until he comes to visit her again that evening.

The emotions of the woman expressed in this poem were probably very common in the case of the "visitation marriage," where the man would go to the woman's house after the sun set and leave with the break of dawn. Some men surely delighted in the custom, but there must have been others, of a more adulterous nature, who resented having the sashes of their robes kept "hostage."

The Korean brocade was an expensive import, so the image of the man here suggests wealth and upper-class status. The poem was perhaps a popular contemporary song added to the Hitomaro Collection by its editors.

臥いまろび恋ひは死ぬともいちしろく色には出でじ朝顔が花

読人不詳

Koimarobi
koi wa shinutomo
ichishiroku
ironiwa ideji
asagao ga hana

I may toss and turn,

but even should I die from the longing

I shall not make it visible, reveal it in clear colors

like the blossoms of the morning glory.

Anonymous

臥いまろび
恋ひは死ぬとも
いちしろく
　色には出でじ
　朝顔が花

13　「ころげまわって片思いに苦しみ、ついにはこがれ死に
してしまおうとも、けっしてありありと表情に出したり
はすまい、あの朝顔のように鮮やかな色には」

　現代人にとって不可解に思える古代人の心理の一つ
に、この忍ぶ恋がある。自分が恋いこがれていることを
当の相手に知られてはならないのである。百人一首式子
内親王の歌もそれで、「玉の緒よたえなばたえねながら
へば忍ぶることの弱りもぞする」。万葉の作者未詳の歌
と式子内親王の有名な歌と、意味するところは同じであ
る。

　これほど強いタブーには、思う相手の名を口にすると
呪いを受けるという強い信仰上の理由があったと考えら
れる。

　　　　言に出でて
　　　　言はばゆゆしみ
　　　　朝顔の
　　　　　ほには咲き出ぬ
　　　　　恋もするかも

　上掲の歌と並んで出ている歌で、「言葉に出していう
ことはゆゆしい大事にもなりかねないから、朝顔の花の
ように鮮やかに色を外にあらわしたりはしない、そうい
ううつらい恋を私はしているのだ」という意味。

I may toss and turn,

but even should I die from the longing

I shall not make it visible, reveal it in clear colors

like the blossoms of the morning glory.

Anonymous

[Volume 10, 2274]

One of the aspects of the psychology of the ancients which contemporary readers find unfathomable is this hidden love. One must not let the object of one's yearning know of it. Such is the famous poem by Princess Shikishi in the *Hyakunin isshu* (One Hundred Poems by One Hundred Poets Collection), in which she says that, rather than having her love revealed, she would let "the thread of life be cut, if so it must."

This anonymous poem from the *Man'yōshū* and the renowned work by Princess Shikishi share the same meaning.

It is thought that behind this powerful taboo was a strongly held belief that to speak the other's name would bring a curse upon the speaker. The above poem is followed by another:

Fearful it would be

to speak it out in words,

so I endure a love

like the morning glory

that never blooms conspicuously.

14

振り放けて三日月見れば一目見し人の眉引き思ほゆるかも

大伴家持

Furisakete
mikazuki mireba
hitome mishi
hito no mayobiki
omooyuru kamo

As I turn my gaze upward
and see the crescent moon,
I am reminded
of the trailing eyebrows
of the woman I saw but once.

Ōtomo Yakamochi

振り放けて
三日月見れば
一目見し
　人の眉引き
　思ほゆるかも

　　　　　大伴家持
　　　　　［巻6・994］

14 「眉月」という漢語がある。眉の形をした月、つまり新月、三日月をさす。

「振り仰いで、空にほそくかかっている三日月を見ると、一目見たあの人の、ほそく尾を引くような眉が思いだされて……」というこの歌、おそらく「眉月」という言葉にヒントを得て作られたものだろう。

実はこれは万葉末期の大歌人家持が16歳当時作った歌で、家持の大量の作のうち年代が明らかな最初のものである。そう知って読むと一層この淡い恋心の歌がういういしく好ましく思われてくる。

万葉ではこの歌の前に、叔母であり、歌の師でもあった大伴坂上郎女の三日月の歌も並んでいる。そちらは三日月のような自分の眉を掻いたおかげで、恋しい人に逢えたという歌。蛾眉、細眉、秀眉、愁眉。眉は生きている。

As I turn my gaze upward
and see the crescent moon,
I am reminded
of the trailing eyebrows
of the woman I saw but once.

Ōtomo Yakamochi
[Volume 6, 994]

There is an expression which comes from Chinese, *bigetsu*. It means "eyebrow moon," i.e., the new moon, the crescent moon. This poem, which refers to the painted, trailing eyebrows of women in the ancient period, was probably composed taking its hint from the word.

This is a work that the great poet of the late *Man'yō* period, Yakamochi, wrote at the age of sixteen. Among the voluminous works of Yakamochi, it is the earliest datable poem. Reading it with an awareness of the author's youth makes this poem of transitory love all the more fresh and endearing.

In the *Man'yōshū*, this work is preceded by a poem on the crescent moon written by Lady Ōtomo Sakanoue, Yakamochi's aunt and poetry teacher. In that poem the Lady tells how scratching her eyebrows brought an encounter with the one she loved. Arched eyebrows. Slender eyebrows. Prominent eyebrows. Knitted eyebrows. The eyebrows are alive.

庭に立つ麻手刈り干し布さらす東女を忘れたまふな　常陸娘子

Niwa ni tatsu
asade karihoshi
nuno sarasu
Azuma-omina wo
wasuretamouna

Do not forget

this Eastern woman,

cutting the hemp

that grows in the garden

and drying it for cloth in the sun.

The Maiden of Hitachi

庭に立つ
麻手刈り干し
布さらす
東女を
忘れたまふな

常陸娘子
［巻4・521］

15 「藤原宇合大夫、遷任して京に上る時に、常陸娘子の贈る歌」として出ている。地方長官（常陸守）として赴任していた宇合が、任期を了えて平城京（奈良）に帰る時、土地の女性が別離を惜しんで贈った歌である。

　宇合という人は並みの官吏ではなかった。父が藤原不比等、祖父がかの有名な藤原鎌足。つまり奈良朝きっての名門の子である。常陸守に任命される直前、2年間ほど遣唐副使として唐にも行っていた。知識人としても一流で、『懐風藻』『経国集』（いずれも漢詩文集）に漢詩が採られている。『常陸国風土記』も彼の在任中に編まれたらしい。

　そういう男の常陸での妻だった人はどんな床しい女性だったのだろう。麻を干し、布をさらして労働にいそしみながら、自らは行くこともない奈良の都をしのぶ「東女」。彼女は自分の労働する姿を歌の中に刻みこんで彼に贈った。宇合がこの歌を大事に持ち返ったおかげで、やがて万葉集にも録されることになった。

Do not forget

this Eastern woman,

cutting the hemp

that grows in the garden

and drying it for cloth in the sun.

The Maiden of Hitachi
[Volume 4, 521]

This appears in the anthology as "a poem sent by the Maiden of Hitachi to her husband, Fujiwara Umakai, when he returned from his provincial post to the capital." It is a poem sent to him by a local woman, lamenting her separation from him when he completed his tour of duty as the governor of Hitachi in the Eastern provinces and returned to the capital at Nara.

This man Umakai was no ordinary official. His father was Fujiwara Fuhito, and his grandfather was the famous Fujiwara Kamatari. In other words, he was the scion of the most powerful family of the entire Nara period. Just before being posted to the province of Hitachi, he had spent two years as an envoy to Tang China. He was also a first-rate intellectual, whose Chinese poems appeared in both the *Kaifusō* and the *Keikokushū*, two renowned anthologies of Chinese writings by Japanese literati. The *Topography of Hitachi Province* also appears to have been compiled during his tenure as governor there.

What sort of charming woman served as the provincial wife of such a man? An "Eastern woman" who, as she engaged in the rustic labor of drying hemp in the sun for cloth, longed for the capital of Nara, where she herself would never go. Etching a portrait of her own labor into a poem, she sent her composition to him. Umakai brought it back with him as a cherished souvenir, and as a result it found its way into the *Man'yōshū*.

16

験(しるし)なき恋をもするか夕されば人の手まきて寝(ぬ)らむ児(こ)故(ゆゑ)に　読人(よみびとしらず)不詳

Shirushi naki
koi omo suruka
yū sareba
hito no te makite
nuramuko yue ni

I have fallen into a yearning
　　with no requite,
for a girl who, when night comes,
sleeps pillowed in another's arms.

Anonymous

験なき

恋をもするか

夕されば

　人の手まきて

　寝らむ児故に

読人不詳
［巻11・2599］

16　万葉集巻4に大伴安麻呂のこんな歌がある。

　　　　神木にも

　　　手は触るといふを

　　　うつたへに

　　　　人妻といへば

　　　　触れぬものかも

　「手で触れたりいためたりすれば祟りがあるというご神木でさえさわることがあるのに、人妻というと、あながちに触れられないというのか」というので、「人妻に触れてなぜ悪い？」という気持ちが主眼であるのは明白。

　万葉時代の男たちが、少なくとも歌に見る限り、「人妻」に対して強い興味と関心を示しているのは面白いことだ。それはひとつには、男と女が結婚しても同居せず、男による妻問い婚の形をとっていたこととも深い関係があろう。わが恋する人のもとへ、今夜も別の男が通っているだろうというこの歌の作者の嘆きは、大勢の男に共感されたはずである。

I have fallen into a yearning
      with no requite,
for a girl who, when night comes,
sleeps pillowed in another's arms.

Anonymous
[Volume 11, 2599]

In Volume 4 of the *Man'yōshū* is the following poem by Ōtomo Yasumaro:

If men can touch
even the untouchable sacred tree,
why can I not touch you
simply because you are another's wife?

It is an interesting fact that men in the *Man'yō* period, at least in their poetry, had a strong interest in and attraction to "the wife of another." One reason for this seems to be that men and women, even if they were married, did not live together, their unions taking the form of "visitation marriages." The majority of men surely shared the lament of this poet that tonight, too, another man was probably visiting his beloved.

君待つと我（あ）が恋ひ居（を）れば我（わ）がやどの簾（すだれ）動かし秋の風吹く

額田王（ぬかたのおおきみ）

Kimi matsu to
a ga koi oreba
wa ga yado no
sudare ugokashi
aki no kaze fuku

As I stay here yearning,

while I wait for you, my lord,

the autumn wind blows,

swaying the bamboo blinds

of my lodging.

Princess Nukata

君待つと
我が恋ひ居れば
我がやどの
簾動かし
秋の風吹く

額田王
［巻4・488］

17　天智天皇の後宮の一人だった額田王が「近江天皇（天智）を思ひて作る歌」とある。額田王の歌はそれほど多く万葉集に残されてはいないが、中でこの歌はその優しい情緒のためもあって、大いに愛誦されたもの。恋人の訪れを待ちかねている美しい女性の面影がある。

　ただし、こういう詞書はどこまで信用していいものかわからない。万葉集の編纂が行われたころには、万葉初期歌人である伝説的美女額田王はとうの昔に世を去っていたからで、この詞書はたぶん編纂者がつけたに違いないからである。額田王は最初大海人皇子（天智の弟、のちの天武天皇）の妻、のち兄の天智の後宮に入ったことから、いろいろ艶めかしい空想を刺激する人だった。

　でも一つだけ確かなことがある。ここでは秋風が主役になっているということ。秋風は、詩というものの中では、思われ人の訪れに匹敵するほどに胸をときめかせる、一つのひそかな「予兆」そのものとして、古代人の肌を敏感に目覚めさせた。

As I stay here yearning,

while I wait for you, my lord,

the autumn wind blows,

swaying the bamboo blinds

    of my lodging.

Princess Nukata
[Volume 4, 488]

A headnote to this work in the *Man'yōshū* tells us that Princess Nukata, who was one of the consorts of Emperor Tenchi, "composed this poem thinking of the Emperor." There are not that many poems by Princess Nukata recorded in the *Man'yōshū*; this is one of her most beloved poems, treasured for its sensitive lyrical mood. Here is an image of a beautiful woman yearning for her lover to arrive.

We do not know, however, to what extent this sort of headnote can be believed. For by the time the *Man'yōshū* was compiled, the legendary beauty Princess Nukata, one of the poets of the early period, had long departed from this world, and the explanatory headnote was attached by an editor at this much later time. Princess Nukata's life was such as to stimulate various erotic fantasies, for she was first the wife of Prince Ōama (the younger brother of Emperor Tenchi, later himself to assume the throne as Emperor Temmu), following which she became a consort of her first husband's elder brother, Emperor Tenchi.

One thing, however, is certain here. And that is that the protagonist of this particular drama is the autumn wind itself. In the realm of poetry, the autumn wind brought as much excitement as the actual visit of the lover. As a secret premonition of someone's arrival, the exquisite touch of the autumn wind awakened the senses of the ancients.

玉垂の小簾のすけきに入り通ひ来ねたらちねの母が問はさば風と申さむ

読人不詳

Come to me,

again and again,

slipping between the jewelled blinds.

If my mother, with her milk-full breasts,

should ask what is that sound,

let us tell her it's the wind.

Tamadare no
osu no sukeki ni
irikayoikone
tarachine no
haha ga towasaba
kaze to mousan

Anonymous

玉垂の
小簾のすけきに
入り通ひ来ね
　たらちねの
　母が問はさば
　風と申さむ

読人不詳
［巻11・2364］

18

　五七七・五七七の旋頭歌形式。五七七ひとつだけの形式を片歌とよぶが、口ずさんで見ればわかるように、片歌だけだと何かしら不十分な気持ちが残る。つまり片歌は、こちらの気持ちを全部言い切らずに相手の答えを待つという時の気分にふさわしい形式。

　旋頭歌はこの片歌を２つ並べた形だから、１首の中で問答しているような歌も多く、それがまたなかなか気持ちのいいものである。ただし、この歌の場合は問答ではない。「玉垂れのすだれの隙間を通って私のところへかよって来てね。お母さんが『なに』ときいたら、『風でしょ』と申しましょう」

　男を誘う女心の歌。当時は母親が娘を厳しく監督していた。男は風になって通わねばならなかった。

Come to me,

again and again,

slipping between the jewelled blinds.

If my mother, with her milk-full breasts,

should ask what is that sound,

let us tell her it's the wind.

Anonymous
[Volume 11, 2364]

A poem in *sedōka* form, with a syllabic rhythm of 5-7-7, 5-7-7, i.e., two triplets. A single triplet of 5-7-7 was known as the *katauta*, the "one-sided poem," but if one actually tries reciting such a half-poem one will sense something inadequate about the form.

The *sedōka* consists of two *katauta*. Many of the *sedōka* consist of a dialogue, and many of these dialogues within a single poem are quite pleasing. But this particular poem is not a dialogue.

This is a poem of a woman's feelings as she entices a man. Girls in this period were under the strict surveillance of their mothers. Men had to become the wind in order to reach them.

彦星し妻迎へ舟漕ぎ出らし天の川原に霧の立てるは

山上憶良

Hikohoshi shi
tsuma mukae bune
kogi zurashi
ama no kawara ni
kiri no tateru wa

It seems that the herd boy

has begun rowing the boat

across the sky to meet his wife:

the mist is rising

on the riverbank of heaven.

Yamanoue Okura

彦星し
妻迎へ舟
漕ぎ出らし
天の川原に
霧の立てるは

山上憶良
［巻8・1527］

19

7月7日（陰暦）の夜、牽牛、織女の男女二つの星が、一年に一度だけ許されて天の川を舟で渡り、一夜を共寝するという中国の伝説。どういうわけか古代日本の貴族社会で大受けに受け、現在に至る七夕行事が始まった。

面白いことに中国では織女が舟に乗って天の川を渡るのである。日本で牽牛すなわち彦星の方から織女に逢いにゆくのは、古代日本の妻問い婚の形式に合わせて伝説を作りかえてしまったのだ。よくあることだが愉快である。

万葉集には七夕の歌が合計132首もある。大した量である。柿本人麻呂のいわば作歌ノートあるいは収集ノートのような性格の歌集と思われる柿本人麻呂歌集から万葉に採られた中にも、秀作が何首もある。古代人は、天体としての星そのものより、年に一度しか逢えない男女にロマンティックに共感したのだった。

It seems that the herd boy
has begun rowing the boat
across the sky to meet his wife:
    the mist is rising
    on the riverbank of heaven.

Yamanoue Okura
[Volume 8, 1527]

There is a Chinese legend that, on the seventh day of the seventh month (lunar calendar), two stars in the sky—one the herd boy and the other the weaver girl—are allowed to cross the heavens by boat and sleep together, their only reunion in the year. For some reason the legend became enormously popular in the aristocratic society of ancient Japan. Thus began the Tanabata Festival, which continues to the present day.

Interestingly, in China it is the weaver girl who rides the boat across the skies to meet her husband, whereas the Japanese version of the legend has the male star, the herd boy, setting out to meet her. The legend was rewritten to conform with the ancient Japanese custom of the man going to see his wife in "visitation marriage." The rewriting of an imported legend is not unusual, but it is amusing.

The *Man'yōshū* includes some 132 Tanabata poems. That is quite a number. There are several masterpieces on the theme among the poems chosen for inclusion in the *Man'yōshū* from the Hitomaro Collection, which is thought to have been a kind of composition notebook of sketches by the great poet Kakinomoto Hitomaro. The ancients responded romantically not to heavenly objects as such, but rather to the male and female stars that could only meet each other once a year.

20

秋風に今か今かと紐解きてうら待ち居るに月傾きぬ　大伴家持

*Akikaze ni
imaka imaka to
himo tokite
ura machi oru ni
tsuki katabukinu*

I stay here waiting for him
in the autumn wind, my sash untied,
wondering, is he coming now,
　　is he coming now?
And the moon is low in the sky.

Ōtomo Yakamochi

秋風に
今か今かと
紐解<ruby>きて<rt>ひもと</rt></ruby>
　うら待ち<ruby>居る<rt>を</rt></ruby>に
　　月<ruby>傾<rt>かたぶ</rt></ruby>きぬ

<ruby>大伴家持<rt>おおとものやかもち</rt></ruby>
［巻20・4311］

20　大伴家持の作とあるが、これは女が恋人を待っていらいらしている歌ではないか。いったいどういうことか──実は家持が「独り<ruby>天漢<rt>あまのがは</rt></ruby>を仰ぎて作れり」と題して作った8首の歌のひとつで、「七夕」の歌なのである。古代の陰暦では7月からが秋。そのため七夕は、秋の到来とともに迎える日本で最も受けのいい行事となった。牽牛星と織女星が、一年に一度だけしか逢うことを許されない仲だというのが、古代人のロマンティシズムをいたく刺激したのである。

　だから、この歌は織女になり代って家持が作った「待つこと久し」の歌。古代の愛人同士は、逢って別れる時互いに下着の紐を結び合い、次の逢瀬までそれを解かないという誓いのしるしとした。その紐を、待ちきれずに自分からほどいて、こんなに待ちこがれているのに……

I stay here waiting for him
in the autumn wind, my sash untied,
wondering, is he coming now,
    is he coming now?
And the moon is low in the sky.

Ōtomo Yakamochi
[Volume 20, 4311]

This is recorded as a poem by Yakamochi, a male poet, but in it a woman is waiting for her lover. What is going on here? In fact, this is one of eight poems by Yakamochi "as he sat alone gazing up at the Milky Way," and is a Tanabata poem. In the ancient lunar calendar, autumn began after the seventh month. For this reason Tanabata— greeting the start of the fall season—became the most popular festival in Japan. And the fact that the herd boy star and the weaver girl star were only allowed to meet once a year enormously stimulated the romantic imagination of the ancients.

Thus, here Yakamochi assumed the emotions of the weaver girl and composed a poem about her "long wait." Ancient lovers, upon parting after an encounter, would tie together the sashes of their underrobes, and pledge not to untie them until they met again. Here the woman, unable to wait any longer, herself untied the sashes, her yearning so intense, but still . . .

このしぐれいたくな降りそ我妹子に見せむがために黄葉取りてむ

久米朝臣広縄

Kono shigure
itaku na furiso
wagi-moko ni
misen ga tame ni
momichi toriten

Autumn showers,

do not fall so hard,

for I would pick the yellowing leaves

and show them to my girl.

Kume Hirotsuna

このしぐれ

いたくな降りそ

我妹子に

　見せむがために

　黄葉取りてむ

久米朝臣広縄

［巻19・4222］

21　この作者は大伴家持が越中守として今の富山県に赴任
していたころ（天平時代）、家持のもとで役人をしていた
人だが、万葉集によると家持とは公私両面でごく気の合
う主従だったらしい。理由の一つは、大勢の下僚たちの
中でも広縄が和歌の作者として最も才能があったからと
思われる。

　この歌も実は広縄の自宅に家持がやってきて宴会をし
た時の歌。ほかにも人はいたろうに、家持は万葉集には
この歌と、それに応じた自作との2首だけをとっている。

　歌の背景には、奈良に妻を置いたまま越中に赴任して
いる広縄の旅愁がある。

「時雨よ、あまり降るなよ、妻に見せてやるために、こ
の美しい黄葉を折り取って送ってやろうから」

　この歌を受けた家持の歌は、黄葉は大丈夫散りはすま
い、というものだが、宴席で詩歌を作り合う風習は、日
本文芸の根雪みたいなものだった。

Autumn showers,

do not fall so hard,

for I would pick the yellowing leaves

and show them to my girl.

Kume Hirotsuna
[Volume 19, 4222]

The poet was an official who served under Ōtomo Yakamochi in the mid-seventh century, when Yakamochi was governor of the province of Etchū (present-day Toyama Prefecture). According to the *Man'yōshū*, the governor and his subordinate got along very well, both in their public roles and privately, as friends. One of the reasons, it is assumed, was that, among the many officials serving under Yakamochi, Hirotsuna was the most talented composer of *waka* poetry.

This poem was in fact composed at a banquet attended by Yakamochi at Hirotsuna's house. Although others were surely present, Yakamochi chose to include in the *Man'yōshū* only two poems from the banquet, the above poem and one of his own works responding to it.

Behind the poem is a sojourner's loneliness on the part of Hirotsuna, who left behind his wife in the capital of Nara when he was posted to Etchū.

The poem by Yakamochi responding to this tells Hirotsuna that the yellowing leaves will be all right, they will not fall. The custom of composing and exchanging poems at a banquet was, for Japanese literary creation, a kind of lingering snow.

ぬばたまの妹が黒髪今夜もか我がなき床になびけて寝らむ

読人不詳

Nubatama no
imo ga kurokami
koyoi mo ka
wa ga naki toko ni
nabikete nuran

Tonight too

does my woman's pitch-black hair

trail upon the floor

where she sleeps without me?

Anonymous

ぬばたまの
妹が黒髪
今夜もか
　我がなき床に
　なびけて寝らむ

読人不詳
［巻11・2564］

22　妻のもとへ行けずにいる男が、ひとり黒髪を寝床にな
びかせて寝ているであろう彼女を思ってうたった歌。
「ぬばたまの」は黒とか夜にかかる枕詞で、この歌と同
想の歌が他にもいろいろある。たとえば、

　　ぬばたまの
　　黒髪しきて
　　長き夜を
　　　手枕の上に
　　　妹待つらむか

　黒髪といっただけですでにある艶めかしい女性の面影
が浮かぶ感性の伝統は、日本の詩歌に一本の太い筋道を
なしている。白髪がまじっちゃいけないのか、と声をか
けたくもなろうというものだが、言葉としての「黒髪」
には、とにかく命が宿っているとしか言えないものがあ
ったようだ。
「黒髪の乱れも知らずうち臥せばまづかきやりし人ぞこ
ひしき」とは和泉式部。
　それを踏んで「かきやりしその黒髪の筋ごとにうち臥
すほどはおもかげぞたつ」と詠んだのは、若き日の藤原
定家。

Tonight too
does my woman's pitch-black hair
trail upon the floor
where she sleeps without me?

Anonymous
[Volume 11, 2564]

In this poem, a man who cannot make his way to his wife's abode imagines her as she sleeps alone, her long black hair streaming over the floor.

Nubatama, literally the "seed of the blackberry lily," which is small and black, is a pillow word, or formulaic expression, that precedes "black," "night," and so on (it is translated here as "pitch-black"). There are various other poems similar in conception to this one. An example follows.

> Spreading her pitch-black hair,
> does my woman wait for me,
> pillowed in the arms
> of the endless night?

In Japanese poetry there is a major tradition of sensibility in which the mere mention of black hair gives rise to a certain voluptuous image of women. One may complain and ask what is wrong with having some gray hair mingled with the black, but the fact is that an expressive vitality accrues to the words "black hair."

The words of the Heian-period poet Izumi Shikibu come to mind: "I collapse in tears, my black hair dishevelled, and I long for the one who had straightened it for me."

And it was a young Fujiwara Teika who, referring to this work, wrote, "As I sleep alone an image of her appears, clearly as each strand of her hair that I once straightened."

たらちねの母が手離れかくばかりすべなきことはいまだせなくに

柿本朝臣人麻呂歌集

Tarachine no
haha ga te hanare
kakubakari
subenaki koto wa
imada senakuni

Since I left the arms
of my mother
with her milk-full breasts,
never have I felt
so very helpless and confused.

From the Kakinomoto Hitomaro Collection

たらちねの
母が手離れ
かくばかり
　すべなきことは
　いまだせなくに

柿本朝臣人麻呂歌集
［巻11・2368］

23　「お母さんの手を離れて以来、こんなにやるせない思い
をしたことは一度もなかったわ」という乙女の嘆きの歌
である。

　なぜそんな心の状態になったかといえば、生まれて初
めて恋をしたからである。古代の妻問い婚の時代には、
生まれた子は母の手もとで養育されたから、血縁意識は
母と子において絶対的に強く、父親はどこの誰かわから
ない、いや、誰であってもよい程度のものだった。

　その証拠に、古代の詩歌で、とくに庶民生活を詠んだ
ものであれば、母と子の強い結びつきを歌ったものはた
くさんあっても、父の子に対する愛を歌ったものは、山
上憶良のような知識人詩人の場合を除けば、さがしあて
るのがきわめて困難なほど稀れである。

　そういう大切な、強い母のもとから一人立ちしてしま
った今、もう私にはあなたしかないのよ、という男への
心からの訴えかけが、この歌の背後にはあるわけである。

Since I left the arms
    of my mother
        with her milk-full breasts,
never have I felt
so very helpless and confused.

From the Kakinomoto Hitomaro Collection
[Volume 11, 2368]

The lament of a young girl. The reason she has fallen into such a psychological state is that she finds herself in love for the first time in her life. In the ancient period, when "visitation marriage" was the custom, a child was raised by its mother. The sense of kinship between mother and child was absolute, for one was not certain who the father was; in fact, it hardly mattered who the father was.

The proof is in ancient poetry where, especially in expressions of commoners' lives, we find many poems on the all-powerful bond between mother and child. By contrast, poems on the love of a father for his children, with the exception of poets of the intellectual class like Yamanoue Okura, are so rare it takes an extraordinary effort to find them.

Behind this poem is an appeal from the heart, an appeal to a man: now that I have left my mother, have given up that powerful bond and stand on my own, you are all that I have in the world.

真木の上に降り置ける雪のしくしくも思ほゆるかもさ夜間へ我が背

他田広津娘子

Maki no ue ni
furiokeru yuki no
shikushiku mo
omooyuru kamo
sayo toe wa ga se

Thick and fast stream my thoughts of you,

like the layers

   of endlessly falling snow

      upon the cedars.

Come to me at night, my man.

The Maiden Osata Hirotsu

真木の上に
降り置ける雪の
しくしくも
　思ほゆるかも
　さ夜間へ我が背

他田広津娘子
[巻8・1659]

24

　ただ単に「木」というのでなく、「真木」という時、いかにも木そのものがすっくと立ちあがるような感じがする。古代人の言葉づかいは立派だと思う一例だ。この語は檜や杉などの優れた建築用材になる常緑樹を称していう。

　そんな樹木の上に雪がしんしんと降り積もる。心に食い入るように人恋しさを呼びさます光景である。

　さてこの作者は、その雪が「頻く頻くも」降りやまぬように、私は片時もあなたを思わずにはいられないのです、夜が来たら訪うてきてください、あなた、と愛する男に呼びかけている。

　歌の構成上では、「真木の上に降り置ける雪の」は「しくしくも」を呼びだすための序だが、単にそれだけのものではない。恋する女にとっては、自然界のすべてがわが思いの鏡。

Thick and fast stream my thoughts of you,

like the layers

   of endlessly falling snow

      upon the cedars.

Come to me at night, my man.

The Maiden Osata Hirotsu
[Volume 8, 1659]

The "cedar" in the original is *maki*, literally the "true tree"—no mere tree. The expression "true tree" gives us a sense of the tree itself standing erect and tall. This is an example of the magnificent use the ancients made of language. This word's semantic range includes both cedars and cypresses, evergreens that make superb construction material.

And upon such trees falls a thick and endless snow. It is a scene of yearning that penetrates to the soul.

Here the poet calls out to the man, saying, just like the thick, unending snows, I cannot keep you out of my thoughts, even for a moment, so come to me, come to me when night falls.

Formally, "endlessly falling snow upon the cedars" serves as a device to invoke the words "thick and fast," but of course the association is not merely formal. For a woman in love, the entire world of nature is a mirror of her own emotions.

25

刈り薦の一重を敷きてさ寝れども君とし寝れば寒けくもなし　読人不詳

Kari komo no
hitoe o shikite
sanure domo
kimi to shi nureba
samukeku mo nashi

Though I sleep

with but a single thin rush mat

　　for my bedding,

I am not cold at all

when I sleep with you, my lord.

Anonymous

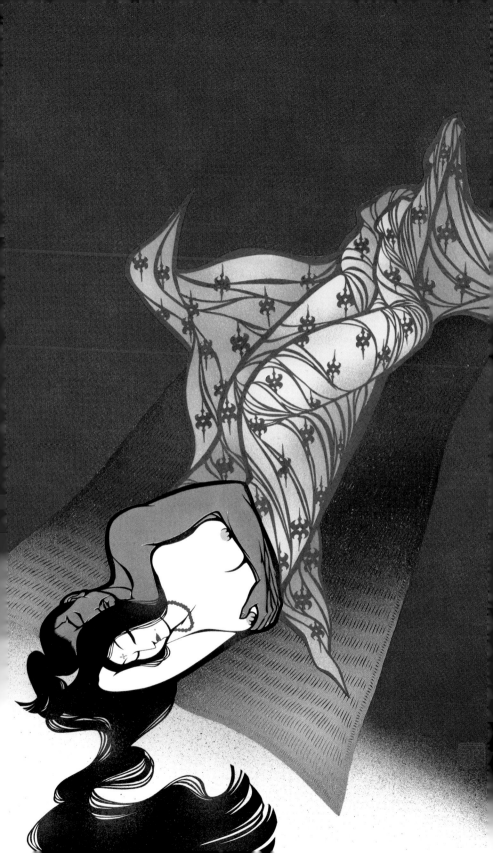

刈り薦の
一重を敷きて
さ寝れども
　君とし寝れば
　寒けくもなし

読人不詳
［巻11・2520］

25　この歌と対照的な意味を詠んだ藤原麻呂の歌がある。

蒸衾
なごやが下に
臥せれども
　妹とし宿ねば
　肌し寒しも

　つまり、蒸すように暖かい寝床、その柔らかい下に寝
ていても、あなたといっしょでないので肌寒くてたまら
ない、というのである。藤原不比等の第四子の麻呂にこ
んな率直な恋歌を作らせたのは、大伴坂上郎女。

　さてこちらの歌「刈り薦の」の作者は、どうやらずっ
と階級も下、つつましい生活を送っている女だろう。
「刈り取った薦の薄い一重の寝床に寝ているだけであっ
ても、あなたと寝ているので、少しも寒くないのよ」

　もっとも、藤原麻呂も坂上郎女とは結ばれていた。だ
から麻呂の歌は、恋人への伊達男のリップ・サービス。

Though I sleep

with but a single thin rush mat

    for my bedding,

I am not cold at all

when I sleep with you, my lord.

Anonymous
[Volume 11, 2520]

There is a poem by Fujiwara Maro which presents an interesting contrast with the one above.

Though I sleep

beneath soft, warm bedding,

how cold my skin is,

for I do not share my bed

with you, my woman.

In other words, no matter how warm and soft the bedding may be, the cold is unbearable when I am without you. It was Lady Ōtomo Sakanoue who inspired Maro, the fourth son of Fujiwara Fuhito, to such a straightforward expression of yearning.

But the author of the above poem, with its "thin rush mat," would seem to be a woman of a much lower class, leading a modest existence.

The fact is that Fujiwara Maro was also a lover of Lady Sakanoue, so Maro's poem consists of a kind of lip service, the type given by a gallant to his lover.

君が行く道の長手を繰り畳ね焼き滅ぼさむ天の火もがも　狭野弟上娘子

O for a heavenly fire!

I would reel in

the distant road you travel,

fold it up,

　　and burn it to ashes.

Kimi ga yuku
michi no nagate o
kuri tatane
yaki horobosan
ame no hi mo gamo

The Daughter of Sano Utogami

君が行く
道の長手を
繰り畳ね
焼き滅ぼさむ
天の火もがも

狭野弟上娘子
［巻15・3724］

26 『万葉集』の中でも有名な女の恋歌の一つ。

作者は男子禁制の斎宮寮に仕える女官だったが、中臣宅守という廷臣とひそかに通じた。露見して男は越前へ流罪の身となる。悲運の男女は互いの安否を気づかい、実らぬ恋であっても、互いの愛の変わらぬことを誓いあう歌を合計63首かわした。これらが巻15に収録されて後世読者の同情共感を集めることになった。うち見たところ、どうやら女の歌の方が情熱的で劇的な点、まさっているように思われる。中でもこの1首は有名だ。

ただ、二人の贈答歌全体が、ひょっとしたら後世のだれかが作ったフィクションだったかもしれないという考えもある。あながちに否定できない説のように思われる。

「道の長手」は男が向かう配所までの長い道。その長い道をたぐり寄せ、折り畳んで焼きつくしてしまう天の火はないものだろうか、ああ天の火よ、と女は悲嘆してうたった。天の火はついにくだってこなかったが、歌は残り、地上から立ちのぼり続けている。

O for a heavenly fire!

I would reel in

the distant road you travel,

fold it up,

    and burn it to ashes.

The Daughter of Sano Otogami
[Volume 15, 3724]

One of the most famous love poems by a woman in the *Man'yōshū*.

The author was a female official who served in the Bureau of Rites, whose precincts were forbidden to men. Nevertheless, she carried on a secret love affair with a minister named Nakatomi Yakamori. Their affair was discovered, and the man was punished by being sent into exile to the province of Echizen. The ill-fated couple exchanged a total of sixty-three poems in which they expressed their concern for the other's safety and pledged that their mutual love remained unchanged even though it could not be requited. These poems were included in Volume 15 of the *Man'yōshū*, becoming the objects of sympathy and identification for later generations of readers. To make what might be a superficial judgement, the woman's poems do seem superior to the man's in their more intense passion and drama. Among them, this poem is especially renowned.

There is a theory which holds that the entire group of poems between the man and the woman are fictions created by someone in a later age. It is a theory which cannot wholly be discounted.

The "distant road" is the lengthy route the man must travel to his destination of exile. The woman cries out for a fire from heaven; she would reel in the road, fold it up, and burn it. "O for a heavenly fire!" she cries. The heavenly fire never came, but her poem remained, rising from the earth like an eternal flame.

妹に恋ひ吾の松原見渡せば潮干の潟に鶴鳴き渡る

聖武天皇

Imo ni koi
aga no matsubara
miwataseba
shiohi no kata ni
tazu naki wataru

Yearning for my woman,
I gaze into the distance
from the pine fields of Aga.
And the crane soars, crying,
across the lagoon at ebb tide.

Emperor Shōmu

妹に恋ひ
吾の松原
見渡せば
　潮干の潟に
　鶴鳴き渡る

聖武天皇
［巻6・1030］

27

「吾の松原」というのは今の三重県四日市付近の海岸の
地名だろうとされる。アガノマツバラは「我が待つ」に
通じるので、初五の「妹に恋ひ」を「吾の松原」にかか
る枕詞と見る解釈もある。それだとこの歌には恋の意味
は含まれず、単に「吾の松原から見渡すと、今まさに潮
干潟に鶴が鳴き渡ってゆく」という叙景歌になってしま
う。

　しかしどうもそれだけのものとも思えない。

大和恋ひ
寐のねらえぬに
情なく
　この渚崎廻に
　鶴鳴くべしや

鶴が鳴き
葦べをさして
飛び渡る
　あなたづたづし
　ひとりさ寝れば

　その他、鶴の声を聞くと独り寝の寂しさがひとしお深
まる思いをうたった歌がほかにもある。空気を裂くよう
なあの鳴き声には、恋の孤愁に沈む男の姿がよく似合う。

Yearning for my woman,
I gaze into the distance
from the pine fields of Aga.
And the crane soars, crying,
across the lagoon at ebb tide.

Emperor Shōmu
[Volume 6, 1030]

"The pine fields of Aga" are thought to be the name of a place located on the seashore near the present city of Yokkaichi in Mie Prefecture. Since the original *aga no matsubara* suggests *a ga matsu*, "I await," the phrase "yearning for my woman" can be seen as a formal device to introduce the place name. Such an interpretation, however, would rob the poem of any sense of actual yearning, and turn it into a mere description of the lagoon at ebb tide.

An interpretation of this sort seems inadequate. There are, for example, the following similar poems:

Longing for Yamato,
I cannot sleep my sleep;
is it right for the crane
to soar by the islet headland
and cry so heartlessly?

The crane cries,
soaring towards the reedy shore;
how helpless I feel
   as I sleep alone.

There are other poems as well in which the cry of the crane serves to deepen the hearer's sense of desolation as he sleeps alone. The sound of that cry, splitting the air, goes well indeed with the figure of a man gripped with the loneliness of yearning.

若草の新手枕をまきそめて夜をや隔てむ憎くあらなくに

読人不詳

Pillowed, for the first time,

in the fresh new arms

of a girl like the young grass:

must there be intervals between such nights,

though there be no disaffection?

Wakakusa no
nii-ta-makura o
maki somete
yo o ya hedaten
nikuku aranakuni

Anonymous

若草の
新手枕を
まきそめて
　夜をや隔てむ
　憎くあらなくに

読人不詳
［巻11・2542］

28　「若草の」はツマ（夫・妻）やニヒ（新）などにかかる枕
詞。「武蔵野はけふはな焼きそ若草のつまもこもれり」
という歌がある。野焼きのころの素朴な恋人たちの逢引
きを詠んでいるが、「若草の」の一語があるだけで歌は
ういういしい情感に包まれる。
　「若草のようにういういしい妻を得て、その手枕で寝ら
れるようになったばかりなのに、どうしてこんな逢うこ
とができない夜なんてものが二人の間に割りこんできて
いいものか。可愛くてしかたがない女なのに」
　歌の意味はこんなところだろう。古代の結婚は男が女
のもとに通う形態だったからこんな歌も作られた。この
男はどういう理由によってかわからないが、妻に逢いに
ゆけないでいるらしい。溜息の歌である。

Pillowed, for the first time,

in the fresh new arms

of a girl like the young grass:

must there be intervals between such nights,

though there be no disaffection?

Anonymous

[Volume 11, 2542]

Wakakusa no, "like the young grass," is a formulaic pillow word used with *tsuma* ("husband" or "wife"), *nii* ("new") and other expressions. There is a poem which reads, "Do not burn the Musashi fields today, for my wife, like the young grass, is secluded there." This is a poem about the encounter of unsophisticated lovers during the season when the fields are burned; the mere presence of the phrase "like the young grass" serves to envelop the poem in an aura of fresh emotion.

In this poem the man has just gotten a new young wife. He laments that there are nights when the two cannot meet, though he is full of affection for her.

Ancient marriage took a form in which the man would visit the woman's abode at night. The custom made this sort of poem possible. For some reason unknown to us, the man is apparently unable to make his nocturnal visitation. This poem is like a sigh.

梓弓引きて緩へぬますらをや恋といふものを忍びかねてむ

読人不詳

Azusa-yumi
hikite yuruenu
masura o ya
koi to iumono o
shinobi kaneten

Brave man like the catalpa bow

that, once drawn,

  does not slacken—

can it be that he is unable to bear

the vicissitudes of love?

Anonymous

梓弓
引きて緩へぬ
ますらをや
　恋といふものを
　忍びかねてむ

読人不詳
［巻12・2987］

29　「梓の木で作った強い弓でも、いったん引きしぼればそのまま緩めもしないでいられるほど立派な男が、さて恋となると、辛抱しようとしても辛抱しきれないものなのか」

「ますらを」という言葉は、強くて心のまっすぐな立派な男をいう。そういう男が、恋という、どこからともなくやってきていきなりこちらに飛びかかる目に見えない情熱に対しては、どう抵抗することもできない所に、古代人は独特の不思議さと面白みを感じたらしい。

「恋」はほとんど生き物なのである。穂積親王にも、家の長びつに錠をして閉じこめておいたのに、恋の奴め、つかみかかりおって、という愉快な歌がある。

　　　　家にありし
　　　　櫃に鏁刺し
　　　　蔵めてし
　　　　　恋の奴の
　　　　　つかみかかりて

　親王は酒席で上機嫌になるとこの戯れ歌を歌ったということが万葉集のこの歌の左註に書かれている。

Brave man like the catalpa bow
that, once drawn,
　　　does not slacken—
can it be that he is unable to bear
the vicissitudes of love?

Anonymous
[Volume 12, 2987]

The word *masura o*, "brave man," refers to a strong and splendid man with a stalwart heart. The ancients seem to have thought it uniquely strange and interesting that such a "brave man" would find himself powerless to resist the invisible passion of love, which sprang suddenly at him from nowhere.

"Love" is almost a living thing. Prince Hozumi authored the following humorous poem on the subject:

I locked and secured it
inside the chest in my house,
but now that rascal love
leaps out at me!

A note to this poem in the *Man'yōshū* tells us that the Prince recited it when in high spirits on a drinking occasion.

人皆は今は長しとたけと言へど君が見し髪乱れたりとも

園臣生羽娘子

Hito mina wa
ima wa nagashi to
take to iedo
kimi ga mishi kami
midaretari tomo

They all tell me

that my hair hangs too long,

that I should put it up.

But I do not care if this hair that you saw

should stay dishevelled.

The Daughter of Sono Ikuha

人皆は
今は長しと
たけと言へど
　君が見し髪
　乱れたりとも

園臣生羽娘子
［巻2・124］

30　三方沙弥という男が園臣生羽という人の娘と結ばれた。沙弥は乙女を熱愛し、乙女も沙弥を恋い慕った。しかし沙弥はまもなく病気にかかり、若妻のもとを訪ねることができなくなった。彼は悲しんで妻に歌を送った。

「束ねて結うにはまだ短かく、結わねば長すぎるあなたの髪。このごろは逢いにもいけないから、さぞやきれいに櫛を入れて整えてしまったことだろうね」

　それに対して乙女が答えたのがこの歌。

「人は皆、髪が長くなりすぎたね、束ねて大人の女らしくおし、と言います。でもこのままでいいの、あなたの見た髪は、あの日以来そのままにしています。たとえ乱れていても」

　ほかにも多くの歌でその実例が示されているが、古代人は次に逢う日まで、髪型もそのままにしておこうとする習慣があったらしい。

They all tell me
that my hair hangs too long,
that I should put it up.
But I do not care if this hair that you saw
should stay dishevelled.

The Daughter of Sono Ikuha
[Volume 2, 124]

A man named Mikata Sami wed the daughter of a person called Sono Ikuha. Sami was deeply in love with the girl, and she too yearned for him. But Sami shortly afterwards took ill, and became unable to make his conjugal visits to his young wife. In his sadness he sent her a poem. The poem was about her hair, "too short to be bound up, yet too long to leave hanging." He said that since he was unable to visit her recently he imagined that she must have put a brush to her hair and straightened it.

In the poem above, the girl responds by telling him that people around her tell her her hair is too long to leave unbound, that she should put it up like a proper young lady. But she insists on keeping it in the state it was the last time she saw him—even if dishevelled.

As other examples of poetry suggest, it was the custom of the ancients to keep their hair in the state in which the lover left it until they could meet again.

朝寝髪我は梳らじ愛しき君が手枕触れてしものを

読人不詳

Asane-gami
ware wa kezuraji
uruwashiki
kimi ga ta-makura
furete shi monoo

I shall not take a brush

to this hair that lies

dishevelled in the morning,

for it retains the touch

of my dear lord's arms that pillowed me.

Anonymous

朝寝髪
我は梳らじ
愛しき
君が手枕
触れてしものを

読人不詳
［巻11・2578］

31 　男の手枕で一夜を共に寝た女が、男の去ったあとの寝
乱れ髪を櫛も入れずそのままにしておこうと言っている
のである。わが肉体に残っている愛の痕跡を、そっくり
そのままとどめておきたいといういちずな女ごころ。

　尤も、美的観点から見て朝の女の寝乱れ髪が長らく鑑
賞にたえうるものかどうか、多少むつかしい問題だろう。
古代の男女の場合、男は明け方暗いうちに女のもとを立
ち去ってしまうから、そんな余計な心配をする必要もな
かったかもしれないが、いずれにしても、櫛ひとつ入れ
るにも、人力をこえたある神秘な力への畏れの思いが伴
っていたと思われる。

　こういうわけで、女は心ゆくまでわれとわが黒髪の乱
れを撫でいつくしみ、恋する男をしのぶのである。

　次に逢う時まで、髪型も変えず、結び合った衣の紐を
解くこともしないという呪術的な習性がまだ生きていた
のである。

I shall not take a brush
to this hair that lies
dishevelled in the morning,
for it retains the touch
of my dear lord's arms that pillowed me.

Anonymous
[Volume 11, 2578]

A woman, after passing the night pillowed in the arms of a man, declares that she will not straighten her hair after he leaves, that she will keep it as it is. The intense emotions of a woman who would keep exactly as they are the traces of love that remain on her body.

From an aesthetic point of view, it is somewhat problematic whether the dishevelled hair of a woman in the morning is worthy of extended appreciation. In the case of men and women in the ancient period, since the man would leave the woman's abode in the dim light just before the break of dawn, that probably was no cause for worry. In any case, even the simple act of taking a brush to the hair was apparently accompanied by a sense of awe at the hair's mysterious power, a power beyond any merely human strength.

Thus the woman strokes her dishevelled hair, and cherishes to her heart's content her own dishevelled state, as she thinks longingly of the man she loves.

Keeping her hair in its unchanged state and keeping tied the sash of her clothing that had been joined with his until their next encounter: the animistic sensibility was still very much alive.

振分の髪を短み青草を髪にたくらむ妹をしそ思ふ　読人不詳

Furiwake no
kami o mijikami
ao-kusa o
kami ni takuran
imo o shi so omou

My thoughts are of my girl:

her hair, parted in the middle,

is too short to be raised and tied

　　like a woman's,

and so in it she bundles green leaves.

Anonymous

振分の
髪を短み
青草を
　髪にたくらむ
　妹をしそ思ふ

読人不詳
［巻11・2540］

32　髪を神秘な生命力の象徴と見なす習性は洋の東西を問わなかった。旧約聖書で有名な怪力の英雄サムソンと愛人デリラの物語などその典型だろう。サムソンはデリラの裏切りによって、怪力の源である髪を切られ、捕われの身となってしまう。

　日本語で「みどりの黒髪」というのも同じこと。ミドリというのは色彩の緑色のことではない。新しく芽生えた命、新芽のことをミドリといったのである。真っ赤っかの赤ん坊をミドリゴというように、ミドリの黒髪も生命の端的な象徴だった。

　かわいい振分け髪が、束ねて結う（「たく」）にはまだ短かすぎる幼な妻、青草をさも毛髪のように束ねて頭に結っているその若妻は、男にとっては胸のときめく生命そのもの。

My thoughts are of my girl:
her hair, parted in the middle,
is too short to be raised and tied
    like a woman's,
and so in it she bundles green leaves.

Anonymous
[Volume 11, 2540]

The sensibility which saw hair as a symbol of the mysterious life force was common to East and West. A typical example is the famous story in the Old Testament of the powerful hero Samson and his lover Delilah. Through Delilah's treachery, Samson's hair, the source of his power, is cut off, and he is captured by the enemy.

Similarly, in Japanese there is the phrase *midori no kurokami*. Here *midori* does not mean "the color green." Rather it refers to new sprouts, to newly sprouted life. As a red-faced newly born baby is called a *midorigo*, so *midori no kurokami*, "fresh black hair," is a straightforward symbol of the life force.

A young wife whose parted hair was too short to be tied like a woman's, and who instead tied bundles of fresh green grass in her hair, made a man's heart throb, for such a girl represented for him the force of life itself.

我が背子に見せむと思ひし梅の花それとも見えず雪の降れれば

山部宿禰赤人

Wa ga seko ni
misen to omoishi
ume no hana
soretomo miezu
yuki no furereba

The plum blossoms

that I thought I would show to my man

cannot be distinguished now

from the falling snow.

Yamabe Akahito

我が背子に
見せむと思ひし
梅の花
　それとも見えず
　雪の降れれば

山部宿禰赤人
［巻8・1426］

33　「背子」というのは女が男に対していう語であるのが普通である。夫や恋人、また兄弟。ただ、古代でもある時期からは、男が親しい友人に対していう時にこの語を用いた例がある。

　山部赤人はもちろん男である。その人の歌に「我が背子」と出てきているのだから、これは男の友人にあてた歌だろうと考えるのが一応妥当か。しかし作者赤人が女に成り代って作った歌と考えてもおかしくはない。日本文学の歴史で、問題としてもおもしろいのは、男が女に成り代って作った作品なら『土佐日記』はじめ数々あるのに、その逆はちょっと例が思いつかないほどだということ。

　白雪の霏々と降る早春の庭で、白梅の花を前に恋人を思い、せっかくあなたに手折ってお見せしようと思った花なのに、あまりに白くて雪と見分けがつきません、と嘆じている歌。作者が男であることを考えの外において読むなら、この歌は女が恋する男に対して媚びの気持ちをもこめて歌ったものと読める。絵にしようとすれば、白の上に白という難しい題材、したがって花の美しさに力点を置くなら、いっそ紅梅にでもするほかない歌である。

The plum blossoms
that I thought I would show to my man
cannot be distinguished now
from the falling snow.

Yamabe Akahito
[Volume 8, 1426]

Seko, literally "brother," translated here as "my man," is usually
used by a woman addressing a man. It is directed to a husband, lover or
brother. However, after a certain point in the ancient period we find the
word also used by men addressing close male friends.

Yamabe Akahito was, of course, a man. Should we assume from his
use of the term "my man" that this poem is addressed to a male friend?
But it would also make sense to interpret the poem as Akahito's
composition in place of a woman. An interesting problem in the history
of Japanese literature is that, although we find many examples of men
writing as women (the most famous is *The Tosa Diary*), almost no
examples of the reverse come to mind.

The poet thinks of her lover as she stands before the white plum
blossoms in the garden; it is early spring, and the snow is falling thick
and fast. The poet thinks: the blossoms I would pick and show you are
so white I cannot distinguish them from the falling snow. If we put
aside the fact that the author is a man, the poem can be read as a
coquettish appeal from a woman to the man she yearns for. If this were
a painting, it would be a difficult composition indeed: white depicted on
white. If one were to emphasize the beauty of the flowers themselves,
one would have no choice but to make them red plum blossoms.

あしひきの山桜花一目だに君とし見てば我恋ひめやも 大伴家持

Ashihiki no
yama-sakura-bana
hitome dani
kimi to shi miteba
are koimeyamo

If just for a moment, my lord,

I could have viewed together with you

the blossoms of the wild cherries

on the foothill-trailing mountain,

would I be caught in yearning like this?

Ōtomo Yakamochi

あしひきの
山桜花（やまさくらばな）
一目だに
　君とし見てば
　我恋（あれ）ひめやも

大伴家持（おおとものやかもち）
［巻17・3970］

34　古代の文人貴族の友情は、ほんとの所はどうであれ、手紙のやりとりで見る限り、ほとんど恋人同士と変らないものがあった。この歌で「君」といわれている相手もそれで、越中守だった作者家持の下僚、大伴池主（いけぬし）がその人。

　家持は当時大病からの回復期にあり、池主との間に綿々たる恋文に似た手紙のやりとりをくり返していた。歌あり漢詩あり漢文あり。

　都を遠く離れた任地で最も貴重だったのは、文や詩で思いを明かしあえる教養ある友だったから、漢学の素養豊かな下役の池主は、家持にとってはまさに恋人同然だった。

　その人から、山に咲く桜をただ一目でもお見せしたいものをと言ってきたのに対し、「一目でもあなたと一緒に見られたら、山の桜の花ごときをこんなに恋しがることもないのに」と嘆いたのだ。

If just for a moment, my lord,

I could have viewed together with you

the blossoms of the wild cherries

on the foothill-trailing mountain,

would I be caught in yearning like this?

Ōtomo Yakamochi

[Volume 17, 3970]

Judging at least from the expressions found in letters exchanged by
ancient literary aristocrats, the emotions of friendship hardly differed
from those of love. Such is the case with the friend, addressed here as
"my lord" (the form of address used by women to men), who is in fact a
subordinate of the author Yakamochi, the governor of Etchū province
at that time, a man named Ōtomo Ikenushi.

Yakamochi had just recovered from a serious illness and was
exchanging missives with Ikenushi as intricate as love letters. There
were *waka* poems, Chinese poems, Chinese prose compositions.

The most precious thing for a man who found himself in the
provinces, far away from the capital, was a cultured friend to whom he
could reveal his feelings in poetry and prose. The subordinate Ikenushi,
with his erudition in the Chinese classics, was indeed a kind of lover for
Yakamochi.

Responding to an expression from that person of his desire to show
him the wild cherry blossoms, if only for a moment, Yakamochi
answers that if he could have viewed those blossoms together with him,
if only for a moment, he wouldn't be sunk into yearning for such mere
flowers now.

あしひきの山椿咲く八つ峰越え鹿待つ君が斎ひ妻かも　読人不詳

Ashihiki no
yama-tsubaki saku
yatsu-o koe
shishi matsu kimi ga
iwai tsuma kamo

I am the wife who chastely remains

as you go out to stalk the boar,

crossing eight peaks

where bloom the wild camellias

of the foothill-trailing mountain.

Anonymous

あしひきの
山椿咲く
八つ峰越え
鹿待つ君が
斎ひ妻かも

読人不詳
［巻7・1262］

35 「斎ひ妻」のイハフは、精進潔斎して人を遠ざけ、接触を避けることだから、斎い妻とは、男との接触を絶って身をつつしんでいる妻ということ。

　さてこの歌は、妻なる女性が相手の男に対して訴えているのである、「山椿の咲く峰々を越えて鹿をとらえようと待ち伏せしているあなた、そのあなたの斎い妻なのでしょうかね、この私は」

　古代の生活では、男が山で狩りをする時には、妻は身を浄め、精進潔斎して男の無事と狩猟の成功を祈ったのだろう。

　ただしこの歌は猟師の妻がうたった歌ではない。比喩としてそういう立場の女を引き合いに出したのである。近ごろちっとも現れない男に対して、女が、いったい私は精進潔斎の身なの、とんでもないわよと恨んでみせたのである。いつの世も変らぬ嘆きか。

I am the wife who chastely remains
as you go out to stalk the boar,
crossing eight peaks
where bloom the wild camellias
of the foothill-trailing mountain.

Anonymous
[Volume 7, 1262]

The verb *iwifu*, which goes with "wife" here, means to avoid human contact and remain alone and chaste. It refers to a wife who keeps herself secluded and pure, refraining from contact with men.

In this poem, such a wife is addressing her husband, telling him that while he is away she remains in a pure state.

In ancient life, when the man set out into the mountains to hunt, the wife would remain secluded and chaste, praying for his safety and the success of the hunt.

But this is not a poem by a hunter's wife. Here the poet is employing the image of such a woman as a metaphor. Recently the man has been neglectful in his conjugal visits. The wife expresses her resentment by comparing herself facetiously to a woman bound to ritual chastity. A lament that perhaps never changes throughout history.

<ruby>宮<rt>みや</rt>田<rt>た</rt>雅<rt>まさ</rt>之<rt>ゆき</rt></ruby> Miyata Masayuki

切り絵画家。1926年東京生まれ。
文豪谷崎潤一郎に見出され、独創の
切り絵の世界を確立。一枚の紙を一本の
刀で切り上げる切り絵の技術と、
その卓越した国際性を高く評価され、
1981年、バチカン近代美術館に
『日本のピエタ』が収蔵される。
1995年、国連50周年を記念して、
世界の現代画家の中から、日本人として
初めて国連公認画家に選任され、
力作『赤富士』が特別限定版画となって
世界184ヵ国に紹介されるなど、
切り絵界の第一人者として世界画壇で
活躍。1997年1月5日、上海から帰国の
途中急逝。代表作に『おくのほそ道』、
『源氏物語』、『竹取物語』などがある。

Cut-out illustrator. Born in Tokyo in
1926. He was discovered by the distinguished writer Tanizaki Jun'ichirō, and
later went on to create his own distinct
realm in *kiri-e* (cut-out illustrations). His
cut-out pictures, made with mere sheets
of paper and a cutting blade, have won
admiration for their exceptional accessi-
bility to people from all countries. In 1981,
his work *Japanese Pietà* was selected for
the modern religious art collection in the
Vatican Museum. In 1995, the bi-centen-
nial anniversary of the UN, Miyata was
selected from among contemporary artists
worldwide to be the UN's official artist,
the first Japanese to hold the post. His
masterpiece, *Red Fuji*, was reproduced in
a special limited edition. Miyata continued
to be actively engaged in international art
circles until his death in 1997. His repre-
sentative works include illustrations for
The Narrow Road to Oku, *The Tale of
Genji* and *The Tale of the Bamboo Cutter*.

<ruby>大<rt>おお</rt>岡<rt>おか</rt></ruby> <ruby>信<rt>まこと</rt></ruby> Ōoka Makoto

詩人、文芸評論家。1931年静岡県生まれ。
東京大学国文学科卒。新聞記者などを
経て現在、明治大学、東京芸術大学教授、
日本文芸協会理事、日本芸術院会員。
1956年第一詩集『記憶と現在』で注目
される。1971年評論『紀貫之』で
読売文学賞、1980年随筆『折々のうた』
(新聞連載中)で菊池寛賞を受賞。
詩作品や、外国詩人らとの共同制作の
連詩の試みは海外でも高い評価を
得ている。
『蕩児の家系』など文芸評論集多数。

Poet and literary critic. Born in Shizuoka
Prefecture in 1931. Ōoka graduated from
Tokyo University. His *Kioku to genzai*
(1956, Memory and the Present) is a volume of poems rich in intellectual lyricism.
Among his other writings are *Tōji no
kakei* (1969, Lineage of a Profligate); *Ki no
Tsurayuki* (1971), a study of the poet who
compiled the *Kokinshū* poetry anthology;
and *Nihon shiika kikō* (1978, Travels
through Japanese Poetry). Japan's most
renowned contemporary commentator on
poetry, Ōoka has published a number of
volumes of *Oriori no uta* (1979– , Poems
for All Seasons), taken from his long-run-
ning newspaper column in the *Asahi
Shimbun*.

リービ英雄 Ian Hideo Levy

作家。1950年米国カリフォルニア州生まれ。
少年時代を台湾、香港で過ごす。
プリンストン大学卒業後、同大学、
スタンフォード大学の教授として、
日本文学を研究。『万葉集』の英訳により、
1982年、全米図書賞を受賞。1967年以降、
日米を往還。1989年、スタンフォード大学
の教授の座を辞し、東京に定住する。
西洋出身者として初めて日本語の
作家となり、デビューし、『星条旗の
聞こえない部屋』(講談社、92年)で
野間文芸新人賞を受賞。
現在、法政大学教授。
著書に『日本語の勝利』『天安門』
『アイデンティティーズ』(以上、講談社)など。

Novelist and scholar of Japanese literature. Born in California in 1950 and
educated in Taiwan, America and Japan.
Graduated from Princeton University,
where he studied and taught Japanese
literature, Levy became Associate
Professor of Japanese Literature at
Stanford University. He received the
American Book Award in 1982 for his
translation of the classic Japanese poetry
anthology, the *Man'yōshū*.
With the publication of *Seijōki no kikoe-
nai heya* (1992, The Room Where the
Star-Spangled Banner Cannot Be
Heard), which won the coveted Noma
Prize for New Writers, Levy became
the first Westerner ever to be recognized
as a writer of original Japanese fiction.

ドナルド・キーン Donald Keene

日本文学研究者。コロンビア大学名誉教授。
1922年ニューヨーク市生まれ。
コロンビア大学で1951年に学位取得。
ケンブリッジ大学、京都大学などでも
日本文学を研究。1955年から92年まで
コロンビア大学教授。
主な著書に『日本文学史』(1976年〜、9冊
既刊)、『百代の過客』、『日本文学の歴史』
(全18巻)などがある。また近松門左衛門、
太宰治、三島由紀夫らの英訳も多数。
日本文学の国際的評価を高めるのに
貢献し、1962年に菊池寛賞、75年に
勲三等旭日綬章、83年に国際交流基金賞、
98年に朝日賞などを受けている。

U.S. scholar and translator of Japanese
literature. Born in New York City in
1922. Keene graduated from Columbia
University, where he received a Ph.D. in
1951 and taught from 1955 to 1992. He
studied Japanese literature at Cambridge
University in England and Kyoto
University. His scholarly publications,
ranging in time from a study of the
Kojiki to discussions of contemporary lit-
erature, have established the foundations
for the appreciation of Japanese literature
in the West. Keene has been awarded the
Kikuchi Kan Prize (1962), the Order of
the Rising Sun (1974), the Japan
Foundation Award (1984) and the Asahi
Prize (1998) for his contribution to the
study of Japanese literature.
Publications include *Travelers of a
Hundred Ages* (1984), winner of the
Yomiuri Literature Prize and the
Shinchō Grand Prize; a four-volume his-
tory of Japanese literature—*Seeds in the
Heart* (1993), *World Within Walls* (1976),
Dawn to the West (2 vols., 1984)—as well
as numerous translations.

対訳 万葉恋歌
Love Songs from the *Man'yōshū*

2000年6月30日　第1刷発行
2004年6月11日　第3刷発行

切り絵　　宮田雅之
解　説　　大岡 信
英　訳　　リービ英雄
エッセイ　ドナルド・キーン
企画協力　宮田雅之アートプロモーション
　　　　　株式会社雅房・瀧愁麗
発行者　　畑野文夫
発行所　　講談社インターナショナル株式会社
　　　　　〒112-8652 東京都文京区音羽 1-17-14
　　　　　電話　03-3944-6493（編集部）
　　　　　　　　03-3944-6492（営業部・業務部）
　　　　　ホームページ　www.kodansha-intl.co.jp
印刷所　　光村印刷株式会社
製本所　　株式会社国宝社